HOWDY!

Welcome to the Circle C. My name is Andi Carter. If you are a new reader, here's a quick roundup of my family, friends, and adventures:

I'm a tomboy who lives on a huge cattle ranch near Fresno, California, in the exciting 1880s. I would rather ride my palomino mare, Taffy, than do anything else. I mean well, but trouble just seems to follow me around.

Our family includes my mother Elizabeth, my ladylike older sister Melinda, and my three older brothers: Justin (a lawyer), Chad, and Mitch. I love them, but sometimes they treat me like a pest. My father was killed in a ranch accident a few years ago.

In **Long Ride Home**, Taffy is stolen and it's my fault. I set out to find my horse and end up far from home and in a heap of trouble.

In **Dangerous Decision**, I nearly trample my new teacher in a horse race with my friend Cory. Later, I have to make a life-or-death choice.

Next, I discover I'm the only one who doesn't know the Carter **Family Secret**, and it turns my world upside down.

In **San Francisco Smugglers**, a flood sends me to school in the city for two months. My new roommate, Jenny, and I discover that the little Chinese servant-girl in our school is really a slave.

Trouble with Treasure is what Jenny, Cory, and I find when we head into the mountains with Mitch to pan for gold.

And now I may lose my beloved horse, Taffy, if I tell what I saw in **Price of Truth**.

So saddle up and ride into my latest adventure!

Andi

ANDREA CARTER AND THE

Family Secret

The Circle C Adventures Series

ANDREA CARTER AND THE

Family Secret

Susan K. Marlow

Kregel Publications

Andrea Carter and the Family Secret

© 2008 by Susan K. Marlow

Published by Kregel Publications, a division of Kregel, Inc., P.O. Box 2607, Grand Rapids, MI 49501.

ISBN 978-0-8254-3365-8

Printed in the United States of America

10 11 12 / 5 4 3 2

To Jessica,
my "cover girl."
Thanks for all the fun we've had
transforming you into Andi.
This one's for you.

Chapter One

UNEXPECTED ENCOUNTER

When twelve-year-old Andrea Carter brought her golden palomino mare to a skidding halt near her favorite fishing spot, she expected to find a bubbling, splashing creek full of trout just waiting to be snatched up for supper.

Instead, she found a dead man.

Facedown, he lay sprawled in the middle of a nearly dry creek bed. Thick, dark mud plastered his clothes and head. One hand dangled limply in a pool of dirty water. The creek, which usually ran strong and fast year round, trickled past the lifeless stranger in shallow, muddy channels.

Andi swallowed her shock and fought to calm her racing heart. She knew she had to dismount and see whether the man was really dead, but she couldn't move. Gripping Taffy's reins, she glanced over her shoulder at the two riders galloping toward her.

This is what I get for always coming in first, she thought. *Next time we race, Cory can win. Let him find the nasty surprises!*

"I'm not going near any dead man—not by myself," she muttered. "You hear me, Taffy? We stay put until Cory and Rosa catch up."

A moment later, Cory reined his chestnut gelding alongside Andi and made a face. "You beat me, but it wasn't a fair race. I didn't see that little gully until . . ." His voice trailed off. "What's the matter, Andi?"

She pointed toward the creek bed. "Him."

Cory's eyes grew round.

Rosa pulled up on her horse and gasped. "*¡Dios mío!*" She crossed herself and mumbled a quick prayer. "*¿Quién es? ¿Qué pasó?*"

Andi shook her head. "I don't know who he is, and I don't know what happened. I—I didn't want to do anything until you got here."

Cory dismounted and tossed his reins around a scraggly branch of a scrub oak. "Let's go see. Maybe he's not as dead as he looks. We should leastways get him out of the mud." He grinned. "I didn't figure we'd be fishing a fella out of your creek today, Andi. I'd kind of counted on trout."

Andi hopped to the ground and tied up her horse. She didn't find anything funny about a dead man half-buried in the creek bottom. She looked up at Rosa, still astride her mount. "Aren't you coming?"

Rosa shook her head. "I will stay with the horses for now."

For once, Andi agreed with her cautious Mexican friend. This wasn't the kind of mess Andi usually stumbled into. Knocking down the schoolmaster during a spur-of-the-moment horse race or breaking a window playing baseball was more her style; even a close call with an unbroken horse, or barging into her brother's law office during an important meeting with a client. But not this. Not finding a *dead* man.

She shivered, in spite of the blistering California heat.

"Andi! You coming?" Cory hollered and clambered down the shallow creek bank. "Hurry."

Andi sighed. "I guess I'd better help him," she said to Rosa. She scurried after her friend and grimaced her way down the embankment through the squishy, stinking mud. Each step sank her deeper into the muck. By the time she reached Cory's side, the legs of her overalls were splattered with mud. She squatted next to her friend and drew in a sharp breath. Close up, the man looked *very* dead. His face was ashen between the streaks of dirt. "Is he . . . is he . . . ?"

Cory shook his head. "Nope. Not dead yet. I shook him, and he moaned."

Andi let out her breath. "That's good."

"But he's in bad shape," Cory said. "There's no telling how long he's been here. A day? A week? He's not dead right now, but he won't last much longer if we don't get him out of the sun and into some shade." He reached under the man's shoulders and yanked. Nothing happened. "He's stuck tight."

Andi jumped up to help, but no amount of grunting and groaning and heaving moved the man so much as an inch. "What're we going to do?" She panted and let the man's arms drop to the ground. "Even with Rosa's help, we'll never get him out on our own. We're not strong enough."

"One of us could ride to your place and bring back some of the ranch hands to help," Cory suggested.

"That'll take too long." Andi glanced up to where Rosa sat in the shade. Her friend had dismounted and was leaning against the trunk of an old oak. "I've got an idea. I'll be right back."

A few minutes later Andi returned, carrying a coil of rope from her saddle, which she thrust into Cory's hands. "Here. Loop this end under his arms and across his shoulders. Then cinch it up." She whistled, and Taffy stepped to the edge of the creek bank. Rosa stood beside her. "Here, Rosa!" Andi hollered and tossed the rest of the rope up the incline. "Tie it around the saddle horn. Then slowly back Taffy up when we say so."

Rosa caught the rope and nodded.

"I'm ready," Cory said from his place next to the unconscious man. He shook his head. "Hope this doesn't kill him."

"We'll go slow," Andi said. She signaled to Rosa, who began to lead the palomino away from the creek. Gently, Andi and Cory placed their hands on the man's limp form and waited. The rope went taut, and the man moaned. Then, with a loud sucking sound, the mud gave way and he slid quickly toward the bank.

"Hold up!" Cory shouted. The rope went slack. "Now pull him along real careful, Rosa." Slipping and sliding, they guided the stranger up and over the creek bank and into the shade.

"I don't think that did him much good." Andi squatted beside the unconscious man and brushed at the caked mud and dirt on her overalls. "You suppose he's still alive?"

Cory dropped down beside her. "Let's roll him over and see."

As soon as they rolled him over, Andi shook him. "Mister, are you all right? Wake up." She waited for a reply, but none came. The stranger lay still as death. "Go get your canteen," she told Cory. "A little water might do the trick. I caught Mitch napping under a tree a few Sundays back and poured a whole pitcher of water over his head. I never saw anybody wake up so fast!"

"Bet he was hoppin' mad, too," Cory said with a grin. He sprang to his feet and retrieved the canteen. "Did you catch it for soaking your brother?" he asked, dropping the canteen at Andi's feet.

"Yep. Mitch tossed me in the horse trough, and that was the end of it." She picked up the canteen and unscrewed the lid. "Here goes." A stream of lukewarm water spilled onto the man's face.

It was a miracle the way the man yelped and tried to sit up. He slapped his hands wildly against his face and sputtered, "You trying to drown me?" His voice cracked, and he fell back with a groan.

Andi sat back on her heels, astonished. "It worked! Even on a half-dead fella."

Cory whistled. "I'll say." He brought his face close to the man's. "You know how close you came to never waking up, mister? We pulled you out of the creek, and none too soon. Another day or two in this heat and you'd have been buzzard bait."

Andi winced at Cory's blunt words. But at least the man was alive. For now.

The stranger rubbed his face, took a deep breath, and sat up. "Reckon I owe you kids some thanks." He studied Andi through narrow, bloodshot eyes and pointed at the canteen. "Mind if I put some of that on the inside?"

She handed it over.

The man bent his head back and took gulp after gulp of water before emptying the rest of it over his filthy head. Then he tossed the canteen aside and ran his fingers through his dripping hair. "Much obliged." He swayed and looked ready to collapse. It was clear that even this short activity had drained him. "I feel like a herd of cattle ran right over the top of me."

"Who are you?" Andi asked. "And how did you end up in the middle of the creek?"

The stranger groaned again as he scooted next to the tree trunk and leaned back. "Name's T. J. Silver. I have no idea how I got here. I don't even know where I am." He looked around. "This California?"

"Yes."

T. J. nodded. "Good. Last thing I remember was finishing up a very unfriendly game of cards with the worst poker players I ever laid eyes on." He settled himself more comfortably against the tree and sighed. "I cleaned 'em out pretty good, but I guess they were sore losers and wanted their money back. I don't recall exactly how they did it, but I think they got it back." He winced and clutched his stomach with both arms. "Something don't feel right."

Andi and Cory carefully pushed T. J.'s arms aside. A bright red streak showed through his muddy shirt. Cory gingerly tugged open the fabric and gave a low whistle. "Boy, oh boy, mister. Looks like somebody sliced you up good. All your moving around must've broke it open."

T. J. dropped his gaze to his stomach and frowned. "Don't remember how that happened."

"How long's it been since that card game?" Andi stared at the bright red wound. It was seeping blood slowly but steadily.

"Wednesday night."

"Today's Saturday." Andi frowned. "No wonder you passed out, riding around like that. You should see a doctor. Fresno's not far—not more than a couple hours."

Cory handed T. J. the bandana from around his neck.

"I don't need a doctor." T. J. took the kerchief with a curt nod of thanks. "I've lasted this long; I'll go on living." He stuffed the fabric inside his shirt and pressed his hand against his belly. "I just need a few days rest and some grub, and I'll be on my way." He closed his eyes and leaned back. "If you'll hobble my gelding, I'd appreciate it."

Andi frowned. "We didn't see any horse."

"He's around here somewhere. Could you do a fella a favor and see if you can find him, Miss—?" He paused and managed a weak smile.

"Carter," Andi replied. "Andi Carter." She nodded to her friends. "And this is Cory Blake and Rosa Garduño."

"A pleasure," T. J. said. "Now . . . about my horse?"

It didn't take long to find the gelding. He was grazing on the parched, brown grass not too far from where his rider had gone into the creek. The horse lifted his head and gave a challenging whinny when the three young riders drew near.

Andi brought Taffy to a stop and started to dismount.

"He doesn't look friendly," Cory warned. "Don't get too close. Just grab the reins and lead him back."

Andi dismounted and yanked open her saddlebags. With a confident smile she brought out an apple and waved it at Cory. "I don't know any horse who'd turn down a treat like this." Cautiously, she approached the large bay gelding. "Easy, fella. Look what I've got for you."

The horse pricked up his ears but kept his distance. He shook his mane, snorted, and took a few careful steps toward Andi. His neck and flanks were dark with sweat.

"Be careful, Andi. Don't spook him."

Andi threw Cory a disgusted look and moved closer. "It's all right, fella." She held out her hand. "Come get the apple, and I'll take you to your rider. Then I'll get rid of that nasty saddle. What do you say?"

The horse walked over and took a bite from the apple. With her other hand, Andi reached out and snagged the reins. "I got him. Let's go."

Cory shook his head. "One of these days you're gonna meet a horse that doesn't like you. Then what'll you do?"

"I haven't met one yet I couldn't sweet-talk into behaving." She gave the bay a friendly pat and mounted Taffy.

"Oh, no?" Cory teased. "What about that wild stallion of Chad's? I seem to recollect hearing about a ruckus out at your place last spring. Let's see . . ." He snapped his fingers. "That's it! You didn't get along real well with that big black horse and you almost—"

Andi bristled. "I don't want to talk about that."

Cory chuckled. "I'm sure you don't."

Back at the oak, Andi loosened the cinch on the stranger's horse, and the heavy saddle tumbled to the ground. Freed at last from his uncomfortable burden, the horse lay down and rolled. Andi grinned. "That feels a lot better, doesn't it?"

"You really gonna stay here," Cory was saying to T. J., "when you're so bad off?"

T. J.'s lips twisted into a lopsided grin. "I don't favor bouncing around on a horse for a couple hours just to see a doc. I'm feeling better already." He turned to Andi, who was at work hobbling the gelding. "I'd be obliged if you let me stay up here on your ranch, Miss Carter. If you really want to play Good Samaritan, you could rustle me up some grub and bring it out here the next few days. What do you say to that?"

Andi traded glances with her friends. It was her decision. After all, it was her family's ranch this poor fellow had collapsed on. Cory lived in town, too far away to be running errands back and forth. Rosa would go along with whatever Andi decided, even if she didn't approve—and she probably didn't, by the look on her face.

"I think you should tell your brothers about this stranger," Rosa said in rapid Spanish. "*Señor* Chad will decide what is best to do."

"Chad's too busy haying to be bothered. Besides, it's just for a few days," Andi replied, her Spanish just as fluent as her friend's. "The least we could do is bring him a few supplies."

T. J. spoke up. "All I'm asking is a little something to hold me over. You can ride by on a fast horse and toss it to me if you're uneasy. I'll be off your ranch before you know it." He lowered his head. "I'd be much obliged if you didn't mention my being up here. Those fellas who came after me the other night might still be in the area and eager to finish what they started."

Andi spilled the contents of her saddlebags next to where the man was seated. A couple of cloth-wrapped roast beef sandwiches tumbled onto the grass, along with a few apples and half a dozen molasses cookies. "I can't promise when I can bring more," she said.

T. J. eyed the food with a hungry gleam and reached for a sandwich. "This'll hold me. Much obliged. You three've done me a good turn. I won't be forgetting it." He bit into the sandwich.

"I'm glad we could help, Mr. Silver," Andi said. "I hope you heal up real fast."

"My friends call me T. J.," he said between mouthfuls.

Andi smiled. "All right, T. J. Take care of yourself. I'll see you later." She grasped Taffy's reins and swung into the saddle. Cory and Rosa joined her, and the three riders headed out.

Andi felt her friends' displeasure at her decision to keep quiet about the man at the creek. A sliver of worry that maybe she wasn't doing the right thing pricked her conscience, but she shrugged it aside. *They're acting like a couple of 'fraidy cats, worried about nothing. What's wrong with being kind to a poor drifter?*

Cory glanced at Andi and shook his head, as if he could read her thoughts. "You're making a mistake, Andi. A big one." He touched his heels to his chestnut's flank and galloped away.

Chapter Two

CORY SPEAKS HIS MIND

A ndi nudged Taffy and went after her friend. "Hold on a minute," she demanded when she'd caught up. Both horses slowed to a walk. "What are you talking about?" She shoved a long, dark braid over her shoulder.

Cory shifted uneasily in his saddle. "There's something strange about that fella back there. He's friendly—no doubt about it—and seems grateful we fished him out of the creek, but . . ." He paused, then blurted, "Rosa's right. You should tell your brothers he's up there in your high pasture."

"But he's afraid those others will find him." She gave Cory a disgusted look. "You were sure eager to help him out when he looked half dead. Now you're acting scared. Why?"

"I'm not scared. I've just got questions."

"What sort of questions?"

Cory pulled his horse to a stop and narrowed his eyes. "All right. Tell me this—how in the world did Mr. T. J. Silver know this was *your* ranch?"

The question caught Andi off guard. She stared at Cory and tried to remember what she'd said to T. J. She'd told him her name and the names of her friends. Had she come right out and said he was on the Circle C? She shook her head. No. It hadn't come up. So how . . . ?

"He didn't even know he was in California until we told him," Cory said, clearly happy that he had Andi's full attention. "Yet he asked if he could stay on your ranch a few days. Not my ranch. *Your* ranch.

For all anyone knows, this could be open range." He gave Andi a triumphant look. "Explain *that!*"

Andi couldn't explain. "I must have mentioned the ranch."

Cory shook his head. "T. J. Silver's hiding something. And the fact that he knows this is your spread isn't the only thing, I bet."

"So what? It's a free country. As long as he doesn't bother anybody, he can hide what he likes. We're just getting him supplies to help him on his way."

"What if he's an outlaw? Maybe he holds up stagecoaches. Or robs banks."

"That's a crazy notion, Cory."

Cory's look turned stubborn. "No, it ain't."

Andi sighed. "Why can't T. J. Silver be what he appears to be—a poor drifter down on his luck and in need of a helping hand? The Bible says we're supposed to help strangers in need, 'cause we might be entertaining an angel unawares."

"T. J. Silver's no angel," Cory insisted. "And while I'm glad we saved his life, it doesn't mean I can't be suspicious."

Andi glanced at Rosa and grew silent. If Cory got it into his head that T. J. was a threat, there was no telling what he'd do or say. He might even tell Chad. Andi certainly didn't want that. It made her feel good to know she'd brought a man back from the very brink of death. She wanted to go on helping him get better. It gave her a reason to ride up to her special place for the next few days.

She decided it was time to change the subject—and fast. "Say, Cory. Why don't you stop by the house and get something to eat before you head home? It's a long, hot ride back to town."

Cory brightened at the mention of food. "That's not a bad idea. Thanks."

Andi grinned at her success in distracting her friend and urged Taffy into an easy lope. She cut through the recently harvested alfalfa fields and leaped over one of the new irrigation ditches that carried water from the San Joaquin River to the thirsty acres of orchard fruit and vineyards. Cory and Rosa hurried to catch up. A few minutes later, they pulled their horses to a dusty standstill in the middle of the yard.

Andi slid from Taffy's back and flung the reins over the hitching rail. Then she glanced around the yard. A number of cowhands were guiding a wagonload of alfalfa up against the hay barn. The sounds of creaking wheels, jingling harnesses, and sharp commands to the horses filled the air.

"Hey, what're you doing back so soon?" Sid McCoy, the Carters' longtime foreman, strolled over and tweaked one of Andi's braids. "I thought we got rid of you three for the afternoon."

"The creek's just a trickle," Andi said. "No fishing today." She shot Cory a warning look.

Sid pushed back his wide-brimmed hat and looked Cory over. "Ever think about hiring on as water boy next summer? It's too much for Rosa's brother to handle alone. I could use another fine, strapping lad like yourself."

"Pa'd skin the hide off of me if I took a ranch job," Cory said. "He needs me to help out at the livery. You know that, Mr. McCoy."

Sid shrugged. "It don't hurt to ask now and again, son."

"I'll work for you, Sid," Andi piped up. "I know all about—"

"If I've told you once, Miss Andi, I've told you a hundred times. Your brothers won't let you work those jobs. No use begging. You'll have to content yourself with other ways to earn your keep."

Andi scuffed the dust with her boot. "It don't hurt to ask now and again." She mimicked the tone the foreman had used with Cory a moment before.

Sid's wrinkled, weather-beaten face cracked a smile. He waggled a finger at Andi. "Enough of your sass, miss. Go on with you now, and stay out of my way. We got about a dozen loads of hay to put up today, and I don't want to see any of those bales landing on you or your friends. *Comprende?*"

Andi nodded.

Sid pointed to the hitching rail. "Don't forget about those horses, either. It's mighty hot." He removed his hat and wiped a dirty sleeve across his forehead. "I'll be glad when this weather breaks and we get some rain." He slammed his hat on his head, gave Andi a farewell nod, and headed toward the barn.

Andi turned away from the hay loading and glanced at the two-story ranch house. With its white stucco walls and red-tiled roof, it sparkled like a cool oasis in the middle of the desert. It appeared the perfect place to rest and relax this afternoon, but she knew that behind those thick, inviting walls lay a beehive of activity.

A nudge from Cory brought her back to the present. "So, are we going to get something to eat or not?"

Andi grinned. "Let's head for the cook shack and see what Marty's fixing for the hands. I don't want to show up at the house just yet. Mother thinks we're catching trout for supper. If she sees me, she'll put me to work squishing apples or some other horribly dull job."

"And *mi mamá* too," Rosa said, clearly enjoying her free hours. "There is always much to do in the big house."

"We can eat with the hands?" Cory smacked his lips.

"Sure," came Andi's quick reply. She turned her back on the house and took off across the yard. As she passed the carriage house, her steps slowed, then stopped. Tied up in front of the building stood a fine buckskin horse hitched to a shiny black buggy. "Somebody's here."

Cory and Rosa stopped beside her. Cory shrugged. "So?" He plucked her sleeve. "Come on. Let's eat."

Andi brushed his hand away and circled the buggy, peering into the seat and scowling. "Nobody told me we were having company today." She shot a troubled glance toward the house, then back at the buggy.

Cory rolled his eyes. "So what? A neighbor came by to talk to your brothers."

"When neighbors talk to my brothers they come by on horseback, not in a fancy hired rig. Take a closer look, Cory. It's one of your pa's rigs."

Cory came alongside Andi and brushed his finger over the lettering of Blake's Livery. "You're right. But I still don't see why you care. Aren't you hungry?"

Andi bit her lip and gave her friends a worried look. "You don't understand. The only person who ever comes calling without warning is Aunt Rebecca. She's famous for her surprise visits. And every time she comes, she tries to talk Mother into sending me to the city for a month or two. She wants to turn me into a young lady and send me to some highfalutin girls' school." She shook her head. "One of these days Mother's going to give in. You can only say no to Aunt Rebecca so many times." She made a face.

"Oh, Andi!" Cory said with a laugh, "Lots of folks hire rigs, not just your rich San Francisco aunt. It could be anyone. Why don't you go up to the house and see?"

From the ranch house came the sudden bang of a door slamming, saving Andi from having to reply to Cory's sensible suggestion. She shaded her eyes and looked across the yard. Chad, her twenty-seven-year-old brother, was striding purposefully toward the barn. "Chad!" she hollered. It would be best to find out what Aunt Rebecca wanted beforehand, rather than stumble into the house unawares.

Chad turned. He gave Rosa and Cory a friendly nod then fixed his attention on Andi. "I'm glad you're back. Saves me the trouble of fetching you home." He indicated the house with a jerk of his thumb. "You'd best go inside. Mother wants to talk to you."

Andi froze. "Is it Aunt Rebecca? Has she come to drag me back to San Francisco with her?"

Chad's face was pale under his dark tan. "No, little sister. It's not Aunt Rebecca. It's worse."

Chapter Three

WORSE THAN AUNT REBECCA

A ndi grabbed Chad's arm. "Worse? What do you mean? If it's not Aunt Rebecca, who's here?"

"Hey, Andi," Cory interrupted, glancing uneasily at Chad. "I think I'll pass up your offer to eat with the hands, and head home." Without waiting for a reply, he turned and scurried across the yard. Rosa trailed behind him, untied her horse, and disappeared into the barn without so much as a good-bye.

Andi scarcely noticed her friends' departure. She shook Chad's arm. "Why does Mother want to see me?" She tried to think of a reason, and what it might have to do with a hired rig from town.

Suddenly, she flushed. "It's not Mrs. Evans, is it? Come to complain about her missing flowers? Whatever she said I did, it's not true. I haven't gone anywhere near her yard since—" She broke off at the strange, faraway look in her brother's blue eyes. "Chad?" She shook him, harder this time. "Tell me what's going on. Am I in trouble?"

Chad sighed and seemed to come to himself. "No. It's nothing like that." He laid an unusually gentle hand on her shoulder. "It's not my place to tell you. If you go in the house and talk to Mother, she'll explain everything." He smiled. "I'm sorry I gave you a start. I'm—I'm sorry about everything." He abruptly turned and walked away.

Andi watched her brother's departure with growing bewilderment. Whatever was disturbing him lay just inside the walls of the house. *Whenever somebody as cocksure of himself as Chad starts apologizing for no apparent reason, it means something's terribly wrong.* She took a deep breath, squared her shoulders, and marched for the kitchen door. *At least it's not Aunt Rebecca,* she told herself over and over. *That's something. But what can possibly be worse than a visit from Aunt Rebecca?*

Pushing the back door open, Andi entered the kitchen. The sharp, sweet smell of simmering apples greeted her. "Mother?" She looked around. Her mother was nowhere in sight. Neither was Luisa, their housekeeper, nor Nila, the cook. Across the room, a huge kettle of apples sat on the cookstove, pushed away from the fire. Dozens of clean canning jars stood empty on the oak table in the middle of the kitchen. A canister of sugar lay open. It was clear something had interrupted a day of putting up applesauce.

The door leading to the dining room burst open and Andi's seventeen-year-old sister, Melinda, hurried in. She was carrying a tiny girl with round, blue eyes and a head full of tangled, golden curls. When the child saw Andi, she popped a dirty thumb in her mouth and buried her face in Melinda's blouse.

"Look, Andi," Melinda said. "Isn't she the sweetest thing you ever saw? Her name's Hannah." She brushed by Andi and set Hannah in a chair. Then she crossed the kitchen, opened the icebox, and pulled out a pitcher of milk.

Andi didn't move.

Hannah reached out her grubby hands and whined.

"Just a minute, sweetie." Melinda filled a glass with milk and carefully placed it in the child's outstretched hands.

Andi watched in astonishment while her older sister hovered over the curly-haired, bedraggled little girl. She had planned to ask the first person she saw what was going on, but at the sight of Hannah, she could only point and stammer, "Who's that?"

Melinda glanced up. "I told you. Her name's Hannah." Then she seemed to notice Andi's disheveled appearance—her muddy overalls and disheveled braids. "You look like you fell in the creek. Did you?" Without waiting for a reply, she plunged on. "You better change your clothes before you meet Katherine. I don't want her to see you looking like a grubby ranch hand. Why can't you ever . . . ?" Her voice trailed off in a weary sigh. "Oh, never mind. Just go upstairs and put on a dress."

Andi stared at her sister. Melinda wasn't usually so bossy. Something must have really gotten her worked up, and Andi didn't have to look far to find the reason—the mysterious Katherine. "Who's Katherine?" she asked, ignoring her sister's orders.

Melinda's cheeks reddened, and she suddenly seemed at a loss for words. "She's . . . she's . . . uh . . ." She hugged Hannah and blurted, "She's Hannah's mother."

"That doesn't tell me anything," Andi said in disgust. "Why is she here?"

"Change your clothes and go into the parlor. Mother will explain." She turned her attention from Andi and steadied Hannah's glass so she could finish the last few drops of milk.

"First Chad. Now you." Andi put her hands on her hips. "Mother will explain what?"

When her sister didn't answer, Andi turned on her heel and headed for the dining room door.

Melinda leaped up and blocked Andi's way. "You can't go in there looking like that. Use the back stairs and go get cleaned up." Her expression softened. "Please." Her blue eyes pleaded for Andi's cooperation, but she said nothing more.

With a resigned shrug, Andi gave in. "All right, Melinda. If it means that much to you, I'll clean up before I meet this Katherine person. Whoever she is, she's sure got you in a dither."

Andi ducked into the narrow back staircase that led from the kitchen to the second floor. She took the steps two at a time and nearly collided with her older brother Mitch, who was passing through the hallway at the top of the stairs.

Mitch caught Andi up and spun her around. "What do you think, sis? Isn't it grand?" He set her down and grinned. Then he ran his fingers through his sandy hair and shook his head. "I still can't believe it. It's a miracle."

Andi backed away from Mitch. Had everyone gone *loco?* Chad was strangely quiet, Melinda was bossy, and Mitch? Well, Mitch was behaving like a giddy schoolboy on the last day of school.

Before Andi could question him, Mitch started down the wide, main steps to the foyer. He ran his hand lightly along the polished banister and began whistling a lively tune. Andi caught her breath. For one horrible second, she thought her brother might leap onto the banister railing and slide the rest of the way. She exhaled in relief when he slowed his descent to a walk and reached the bottom of the stairs.

Shaking her head, Andi entered her room and peeled off her filthy overalls and shirt. She tossed them beside the door and threw open her wardrobe. *A dress. On a Saturday afternoon. To meet a stranger everybody's all fired up about. I wish I'd stayed at the creek. No, somebody would have fetched me home. Oh, I wish I knew who this Katherine person is.*

Her thoughts tumbled one on top of the other as she pulled a simple, calico-sprigged cotton dress over her head and struggled to button it up. Her fingers fumbled at the task, and she wondered—not for the first time—whose silly idea it was to design a dress with buttons down the back. *One of these days,* she thought impatiently, *I'm going to button my dress up the front and who cares if it's backward?* With a defiant tug, she tied the wide blue sash, hurried to her vanity, and glanced in the mirror.

Uh-oh. Her face was sunburned and dotted with splatters of dried mud. For the first time since leaving the creek, she looked at her hands. Not only were they dirty, but also smeared with streaks of old blood—T. J. Silver's blood. Andi suddenly felt grateful for Melinda's insistence that she clean up.

She scrubbed her hands and face until the water in the porcelain bowl turned black. Then she quickly plaited her dark hair into two fresh braids, took a deep breath, and decided it was time to find out what was going on. With her heart in her throat, she left her room and headed for the stairs.

When Andi reached the parlor, she stopped short of the doorway. A soft murmur of voices came from the room, but she couldn't make out what they were saying. The door stood open, making it easy for Andi to enter. But she didn't. She stood on the threshold and waited for her mother to invite her in. While she waited, she took the opportunity to observe the young woman sitting on the settee.

Andi's first thought was, *She's pretty—or she would be if she smiled.* She had wide blue eyes, a pert little nose, and a strong chin that suggested this young woman knew how to take care of herself. An abundance of thick, dark curls were pulled back into a tired-looking chignon off her neck. A few rebellious strands of hair had escaped and lay curling around her face. Yet, in spite of her attractive features and outward appearance of self-reliance, Andi sensed an air of weariness and uncertainty surrounding this stranger. She continually clasped and unclasped her hands in her lap and adjusted the folds of her tattered skirt.

To Andi's astonishment, Mother reached out and took the woman's hands. She brought them to her lips and brushed them with a tender kiss. The woman's shoulders shook, and she began to sob in earnest. Andi quickly dropped her gaze when she realized she was spying on her mother and a person in obvious distress. She'd best make herself known before it went on any longer.

"Mother?"

Both women glanced up.

"You wanted to see me?"

"Indeed I do." Elizabeth Carter rose from her place and greeted Andi with a smile that lit up her face. "Come in." She wrapped an arm around her daughter's waist and drew her into the parlor. "Let's sit down, shall we?" She turned to the young woman. "Katherine, this is Andrea."

Andi slowly found her seat. She couldn't pull her gaze from the stranger sitting across from her. Up close, she was even more striking.

Katherine gave Andi a tiny smile. "Hello, Andrea. It's been a very, *very* long time since I saw you last."

Andi looked at her mother for an explanation.

"Sweetheart," Elizabeth said in a shaky voice, "this is Katherine . . . your sister."

Chapter Four

BETRAYED

Andi reeled at her mother's words. She leaped from the settee with a pounding heart and gaped at Katherine. "My *what?*"

Her sister? Impossible. She couldn't have lived her entire life without knowing she had another sister. The idea was ridiculous. If it were true, surely someone would have told her. "No," she said, shaking her head. "It isn't true. I just saw Chad and Melinda. They didn't say anything. Neither did Mitch. They—"

"I wanted to tell you myself," her mother explained. "I thought it would be easier for you to accept the news from me, rather than hearing it from the others." She patted the seat next to her. "Sit down and I'll explain."

Andi backed away toward the door. Her heart hammered against her chest. "You never told me," she whispered, dazed. "All these years and you never told me. Why?"

Before her mother could answer, the sound of running footsteps and an earsplitting shriek echoed from the hallway outside the parlor.

"Mama!" A small, brown-haired girl about six years old hurled herself through the doorway and slammed into Andi. Together they went tumbling to the parlor floor. Behind the screeching child came a boy a few years older. His face was contorted in rage. He clenched his fists and threw himself onto the little girl, who was struggling to right herself.

Andi yelped when the boy's weight fell on her. She grabbed him by his flailing arms and tried to toss him aside, but he was too strong.

A fist connected with her chin. She clenched her jaw in pain and fury.

"Levi! Betsy!" Katherine shouted. "Shame on you! Get up this instant." Neither child paid her the slightest attention, but continued to scuffle. Andi was caught in the middle.

Finally, Elizabeth waded into the fray and helped Katherine pull the children apart. Andi struggled to her feet, breathing heavily. Her mind whirled. She glanced from the two howling children to their mother, who looked ready to cry. Andi could understand that. She was close to tears herself.

"Mother." A new voice joined the commotion. It was Melinda. She appeared in the doorway, looking frazzled. A weeping Hannah hung around her neck. "The children got away from me. I didn't mean for them to interrupt you. I'm sorry."

Elizabeth crossed the parlor and took the crying toddler from Melinda. "It's all right, darling. These things happen." She turned to Andi. "Andrea. I'm sorry. Why don't we sit down and—"

"No!" Andi shouted over the din. Seeing the shocked look on her mother's face, she took a deep breath. "I mean, I can't right now. I've got to look after Taffy. I left her tied up outside, and Sid told me to take care of her." She turned to Katherine, who looked incapable of coping with the two fussing children by her side. Andi wanted to say something to the young woman, something kind, but her throat tightened and she couldn't speak. Instead, she turned and fled.

"Andrea!" Elizabeth's voice echoed in Andi's ears as she raced out of the parlor and into the hallway. "Come back."

Andi was out of the house and halfway across the yard before she realized it was the first time she'd ever disobeyed a direct command from her mother.

Andi leaned her forehead against Taffy's saddle, squeezed the leather in a crushing grip, and shook. She wanted to scream, but that would draw all kinds of unwanted attention from the busy cowhands. They'd rush over, demanding to know how badly she was hurt—for wasn't that the only fit reason for screaming? When they realized she wasn't snake-bit or bleeding to death, they'd scold her and head back to work. So Andi clamped her mouth shut and screamed on the inside.

Katherine! My sister? No! It can't be. How could Mother keep such a secret from me? How could the boys and Melinda betray me like this? Her anger flared. It wasn't easy being the youngest in a busy ranching family. Too often she felt left out of things. But to grow up without knowing she had another sister? That hurt worst of all.

Andi pounded a fist against the saddle. "I've got to find out how this happened." She raised her head and looked back at the house. "I can't go inside. There's too much commotion. Maybe Chad or Mitch?" She glanced toward the barn and quickly ruled out that option. Her brothers were in the middle of an important hay harvest. It wasn't likely either one of them would drop everything to explain to her why a missing part of their family had suddenly turned up—no matter *how* sorry Chad had sounded earlier.

"I'll go to town." Andi perked up. She gathered the reins and mounted Taffy, tucking her skirt in around her legs. "Justin will tell me."

Andi was certain her oldest and favorite brother would be willing to spare a few minutes from his busy schedule to listen to her. Ever since their father had died in a tragic fall from his horse almost seven years ago, Justin had taken over as Andi's confidant and advisor.

Relieved at the opportunity for action, she urged her palomino mare into an easy, loping gait, one Taffy could maintain all the way to town. At that pace, it would take less than an hour to reach Fresno—more than enough time to ponder this new and unasked-for complication in her young life.

When Andi reached Tulare Street, she tied Taffy to the hitching rail and paused before stepping onto the raised wooden sidewalk in front of Justin's law office. She wondered if he would welcome her this afternoon or scold her for coming into town on her own, without permission.

"I deserve to be scolded," she said sourly. "I didn't tell a soul where I was going." Her long ride into town had not only given her an opportunity to think about Katherine, but also time to reflect on what would most likely happen when her mother discovered she'd taken off. None of her reflections had a happy ending.

"Andi!" Cory's loud shout brought her around. He clomped up the boardwalk and stopped directly in front of her, breathing hard. Shoving his straw-colored hair from his forehead, he blurted out his news. "I saw you ride past the livery and figured you were going to see your brother." He gave her a wide grin. "Guess what! I asked Pa if he knew who hired the rig out to your place. He told me it was a young woman named Katherine Swanson."

"I know. I met her." She started to brush by him. "I'm in a hurry, Cory. Good-bye."

Cory reached out and grabbed her arm. "Hold on, Andi. There's more. Did you know she left her baggage at the depot? She asked Pa to wait, and if she sends word, to fetch it from the stationmaster and haul it out to your place. Does that mean she's fixin' to stay awhile?"

"I don't know." She shrugged. "Maybe."

"Who is she, anyway?"

Andi gave Cory a long, unreadable look and said nothing.

Cory's shoulders slumped. "All right, then. Don't tell me. It's none of my business." He grunted, shoved his hands in his pockets, and sauntered off down the boardwalk. "Who cares, anyway?" he threw over his shoulder. Then he turned the corner and disappeared.

Andi clenched her fists. She wanted to slap Cory. "For what?" she asked aloud. Her fists dropped to her sides. "For being curious?" She took a deep breath and opened the door to her brother's law office.

The outer office and waiting room were large and elegant with polished wood walls, a number of bookshelves, and several pieces of expensive leather furniture resting on a thick carpet. Stained-glass gas lamp fixtures hung over cherrywood tables, where the latest editions of the *Morning Republican* and the *Fresno Weekly Expositor* newspapers lay. The office smelled faintly of rich leather and cigars.

Andi glanced around the room. It was deserted. She tiptoed over to Justin's private office and listened. A steady murmur of voices drifted through the heavy, wood-paneled door. She had raised her hand to knock, when the door cracked open. Andi jumped back, out of the way. She scrambled over to a waiting chair, threw herself into it, and snatched up the *Expositor*.

"I'll get right on it, Mr. Carter." Tim O'Neil, Justin's clerical assistant, passed through the doorway, his arms full of documents. Reaching out carefully with his free hand, he shut the door and headed to his desk.

Andi put down the newspaper, stood up, and strolled across the room. "Hello, Tim."

Tim jumped at her voice and whirled around. Papers flew from his arms. He glared at her. "Has no one ever told you it's not polite to sneak up on people?"

"I'm sorry." She crouched down and began scooping up the scattered papers. "I'll help you pick up."

"These are important documents, Miss Carter. I'll tend to them." He sighed. "What do you want?"

Andi stood. She surveyed the heap of legal papers at her feet and bit her lip. "I want to see Justin."

Tim returned to his desk near the door, opened a ledger, and ran his finger down the page. "You don't appear to have an appointment."

Andi spread her hands in frustration. "I'm his sister. I don't need an appointment."

Tim shook his head. "I'm afraid you do today. Your brother has a full schedule this afternoon and cannot be bothered with interruptions."

"I'm sure he'll make an exception. At least tell him I'm here."

With a stiff nod that clearly showed his disapproval, Tim stepped carefully around the mess on the floor and rapped softly on the door to Justin's private office. Then he disappeared inside. When he returned, a look of unhappy defeat covered his face. "Mr. Carter can give you a few minutes. But *only* a few minutes."

"Thank you," Andi replied with a relieved sigh. She crossed the room quickly and opened the door.

Justin's private office was half the size of his outer one, but just as richly furnished. The entire back wall consisted of a huge bookcase stacked nearly to the ceiling with law books. Others lay open on his desk. Piles of papers and official-looking documents lay strewn above, below, and around the books.

Justin rose from behind his desk and smiled. "Andi! What a pleasant surprise on a dull Saturday afternoon." He seemed pleased to see her.

"Tim says you're real busy."

"Not so busy that I can't stop and visit with my sister for a few minutes. Did Mother or Melinda come along?" He brought a chair around. "Sit down, honey."

"I"—she fell into the chair—"I came to town alone." She lowered her head to avoid her brother's gaze.

"Oh?" Justin lost his smile. He returned to his desk, sat down, and gave Andi his full attention. "It must be serious."

Andi raised her head. "I had to talk to you. It couldn't wait."

"What seems to be the trouble?"

She took a deep breath and blurted out, "I want to know about Katherine."

Justin gaped at her.

Andi stared back. She was afraid to say anything more. The look of shock on her brother's face convinced her that she had opened her mouth and made one of the biggest mistakes of her life.

Chapter Five

JOURNEY INTO THE PAST

Without a word, Justin rose from his chair and turned to gaze out the window. For a full minute he stood there, hands clasped tightly behind his back, unmoving.

The long silence, and the way her brother remained motionless, frightened Andi. It appeared as if he'd forgotten she was in the room. She groaned inwardly. *Maybe coming to town wasn't such a good idea, after all.* Aloud, she said, "I—I'm sorry, Justin. I didn't mean to upset you or anything." She rose to leave. "I guess I'd better go home."

"What?" Justin spun around. He looked dazed. "No . . . no . . . it's all right." He returned to his seat and motioned her to sit down. "I'm sorry, but you gave me quite a start. It took me a few moments to collect my thoughts." Then he smiled. "Why don't we start over? Tell me. What exactly would you like to know about our sister?"

Andi plopped into the chair and stared at her lap. "So, Katherine really is our sister."

"Yes."

Andi sighed. She knew her mother hadn't lied to her, but hearing it from Justin made it real. For the second time that afternoon, she felt the sting of betrayal. "You never told me," she accused, snapping her head up and glaring at Justin. "*Nobody* ever told me. Why?"

"That was Father's decision." Justin's tone was regretful.

"Father's decision? But why? Why didn't he want me to know?"

Justin took a deep breath and leaned back in his chair. "You were so little—not much more than a baby—young enough to forget Katherine." He caught Andi's gaze and held it. "It would be best," he suggested softly, "to leave it that way."

"What? Why? What did she do that was so bad?"

"Why are you asking?"

"Mostly because I'm tired of being left out. I'm not a baby any longer, Justin. I'm twelve years old. Old enough to know things about our family, like who this mysterious Katherine is, why she left, and"—Andi paused—"why she's come back."

Justin, who was leaning back in his chair and listening with his usual patience, sat bolt upright. "What did you say?"

"I said Katherine's out at the ranch. Chad acts like he's sorry about something, Melinda's bossing me around, and Mitch—" Andi cringed at the memory. "Mitch squeezed the breath out of me and nearly slid down the banister in his excitement. Mother introduced me to Katherine and I . . . I . . . ." She shrugged. "I acted like a lunatic and ran out the door. So now I've probably upset Mother. Please, Justin. You've got to tell me what's going on."

Justin waved Andi's recital to a stop. "Katherine's here? At the ranch?" He pushed back his chair and leaped to his feet.

Andi watched, openmouthed, as her usually composed and level-headed brother tore across the room and yanked open the door. "Tim, take the rest of the day off. I'm going home."

"Mr. Carter!" Tim threw Andi a look of annoyance, as if he suspected this was somehow her fault. "This is the only opportunity you have to catch up on all those—"

Justin cut him off. "It can't be helped. I'll try to sort through it next week." He grabbed his hat and turned to his bewildered sister. "Come on, Andi. We're going home."

"But, Justin," Andi protested feebly as she followed her brother out of the office and into the late afternoon sun, "you haven't told me anything."

"I'll tell you on the way home," he promised. "You're right. It's time you learned the Carter family secret."

Andi waited on pins and needles for Justin to keep his promise. The buggy, with Taffy tied securely behind, had left Fresno ten minutes ago, and Andi now simmered with impatience and curiosity. Just when she thought she might explode, Justin said, "I'm not certain where to begin, or how much Mother wants you to know."

"Pretend you're Father," Andi suggested with a grin. "You've been doing that for a long time now. Tell me what he'd say."

"He didn't want you to know *anything*," Justin reminded her.

Andi's heart sank. "All right, then. Tell me where Katherine . . . fits in."

"She comes between Chad and Mitch."

Andi waited for more, but Justin remained quiet. This was not how she imagined him telling her about her unknown sister. "Where has she been for the past"—she turned a questioning look on him—"ten years?"

Justin sighed. "I don't know." He clicked his tongue at the horse and slapped the reins. "Get along, Pal." Pal broke into a fast trot.

Andi bit her lip. Getting Justin to talk about Katherine was proving harder than convincing her mother to let her go on a cattle drive. "Justin," she finally said, "you promised. Are you going to tell me or not?"

A minute passed. Then Justin took a deep breath and began to tell her the story. He told her about a girl who was loved by her parents and adored by her brothers. "She was the only girl for quite some time," Justin said, "and a spoiled little thing she was. She became more self-willed and dissatisfied with the ranch as she grew older. Nothing made her happy. She hated the dust, the heat, the cattle, and the work. Most of all, she hated living so far from civilization. She'd had a taste of the city, and her heart yearned for the excitement she believed was there."

"But, Justin! Town's only an hour away. That's not so far."

Justin smiled patiently. "When Katherine was your age, there was no railroad, no Fresno. There was only a little town up in the hills."

"You mean what's left of that old ghost town along the river?"

"That's the one. I'm afraid tiny Millerton couldn't supply Katherine with the social life she longed for. She wanted to live in San Francisco with Aunt Rebecca. Father said no. Kate was barely fifteen—too young and headstrong to go gallivanting off to the city with only a spinster aunt to look after her. Father knew Rebecca wouldn't be able to control her."

"What happened?"

Justin shrugged. "She went anyway."

"To San Francisco?" Andi was stunned.

Justin nodded. "We didn't know where she'd gone until Aunt Rebecca wired and assured us that Katherine was safe and staying with her." Justin slowed Pal to a walk and turned the reins over to Andi.

"Father was furious, but he gave in and let her stay," Justin continued, leaning back in the buggy. He looked tired and sad. "A few weeks later, another telegram arrived from Rebecca, pleading with us to come get Katherine. She had fallen in with 'unprincipled company'—that's what Rebecca called it—and she was afraid Katherine would get into trouble. So Father went to San Francisco and brought her home. Kate never forgave him for that."

"This is terrible," Andi said, shaking her head.

"Yes," Justin agreed. "And very, very sad. Katherine was Father's favorite, but they were too much alike, and always clashing. The more he tried to restrain her, the worse she behaved. The house was forever in an uproar. Then suddenly, for a few weeks, Katherine settled down. She started being helpful—playing with you and Melinda, being pleasant at mealtimes. Mother was radiant. She thought her stubborn, self-willed daughter was finally growing up."

"But . . . ?" Andi prompted.

"But it was only the calm before the storm. Father didn't realize until too late that Katherine's new attitude was a sham. I think he wanted to believe she'd given in, and we could have some peace at last." Justin sighed. "Looking back, I should have known better. I knew my sister well. It wasn't like Kate to be so cooperative for no reason. I guess I was the only one not surprised when Father discovered that she was secretly meeting with a young man. Worse, he was a man who had a bad reputation with women."

Andi's mouth fell open.

"The storm that raged when Father confronted Kate was terrible. I never saw him so angry, frustrated, and helpless as I saw him that day. He didn't know what to do with her. Forbidding her to see Troy would never work, so he locked Kate in her room until he could calm down long enough to talk things over with Mother." Justin's voice dropped to a whisper. "It was the last time any of us saw her. The next morning we found an open window, an empty room, and a note that said she had the right to live her own life, and she never wanted to see any of us again."

Justin drew a deep breath and finished his sad tale. "When Kate disappeared, she took part of Mother's heart with her and left Father a bitter and broken man. He was in such pain over losing Kate that he refused to allow her name to be spoken. No one argued. It was almost a relief to have her gone. Chad, in particular, didn't care if he ever saw her again. Under all his bluster, our brother has a tender heart. He'd been hurt the most by the turmoil and seemed glad it was finally over." He paused again. "Mother grieved a long time over Katherine, but eventually our family began to heal. That was ten years ago. We never heard from her, until—apparently—now."

Andi threw aside Pal's reins and burst out, "How could she just leave? She had *everything*. How could she be so selfish and hurt Mother and Father like that? I hate her!"

Justin picked up the reins and cleared his throat uncomfortably. "Before you judge her too harshly, honey, you better take a look at your own actions. You also have everything. Yet last spring you took off and were gone for three long, frightening weeks. Think how that must have hurt Mother. When she cried for you, she must have wondered if she'd lost you like she'd lost Katherine."

Andi bowed her head in sudden, remembered shame. She knew good and well how selfish she felt at times, especially when things weren't going the way she figured they should. This afternoon's un-authorized visit to town was a perfect example. She'd thought only of herself when she'd ignored her mother's call to come back.

Justin nudged her. "Are you all right?"

Andi clenched her fists in her lap. *No, I'm not all right,* she wanted to shout. Instead, she took a deep breath, raised her head, and looked into her brother's face. "Didn't anyone ever think I might want to know about this?"

"As long as Father was alive, no one dared talk about Katherine. After he died, I made an attempt to find her, but it had been too long. She'd disappeared." He picked up one of Andi's hands and squeezed it. "Mother always intended to tell you. She was just waiting until you were a little older. I guess we figured there was no hurry, since it was unlikely Kate would ever return." He sighed. "I'm sorry, honey."

Andi wasn't quite ready to forgive him. "You're sorry. Chad's sorry. Everybody's sorry, but it doesn't change the fact that I'm always get-ting left out of things."

Justin didn't reply, and they passed the last few miles home in gloomy silence.

"Justin," she finally said as they pulled into the yard, "why do you suppose she's come home?"

"I have no idea."

"What if she's here to stir up trouble?"

"Don't be silly," he said, bringing Pal to a stop. But Andi caught the slight frown that creased his forehead, and she knew he was thinking the same thing. More than ever, she wished she'd never heard of Katherine. Why did she have to come back and throw everything into a muddle?

A smiling ranch hand hurried over. "You heard the news, *señor?*" He untied Taffy from the buggy. "Your sister returns and is up at the house."

As quickly as the passing of a summer storm, Justin's worried expression changed to one of excitement and anticipation. "I heard the news, Diego." He climbed from the rig. "Andi rode into town to tell me."

Diego nodded and tugged on Taffy's reins. "It is a happy day for the *señora*, no?"

"Indeed it is."

Andi jumped from the buggy and halfheartedly followed Justin up the steps to the veranda. She wasn't anxious to become acquainted with her new sister, but Justin certainly looked eager. He opened the door and waited for Andi to enter ahead of him.

She glanced around the spacious foyer and let out a sigh of relief. Her mother wasn't waiting to pounce on her for her recent behavior. It gave Andi a few minutes to collect her emotions and think about what she would say when she saw Katherine. *For Mother's sake, I'll be polite,* she thought, *but nobody can make me like her.*

A slow, simmering anger gnawed at her stomach. She wasn't about to welcome Katherine home with open arms. Because of this selfish, spoiled, older sister's unexpected return, Andi's world had turned upside down. And those three howling kids? Her jaw still ached where the boy had punched her.

Her mother's melodious voice broke into Andi's thoughts like a pleasant, tinkling chime. "Justin, I'm so glad you're home." She glided across the floor with the charm and elegance of a gracious hostess. She could easily have been dressed in a silk evening gown instead of the simple calico work dress and apron she was wearing. Her long, blonde hair lay coiled in a neat braid at the nape of her neck.

Justin greeted his mother with a kiss on the cheek. "Must be an applesauce day."

"It was for a while. Luisa and Nila took over." She turned to Andi and frowned. "You've been with Justin?"

Andi nodded.

"That's a relief. You disappeared—again. This must stop, Andrea."

"Yes, Mother," Andi said. "I'm sorry." She was secretly relieved at the mild rebuke. It appeared as if her mother had more important things to do at the moment than scold her.

Elizabeth nodded. Her smile returned. She took Justin's hands and held them tightly in her own small hands. "Andrea told you?"

Justin nodded. "I came home as soon as I heard."

"This is a happy day, Justin. The happiest day of my life." Like a young girl, she spun around and called up the stairs. "Katherine! Justin's home. Andrea too. Come down."

Melinda leaned over the balcony railing. "She's coming."

Katherine appeared at the top of the stairs. Her hair was freshly combed, and she'd changed into a clean dress that Andi recognized as one of Melinda's. Her eyes lit up at the sight of her brother. "Justin! You haven't changed a bit."

Justin greeted her with a warm smile. "*You've* changed. You're prettier than ever. It's good to see you."

Katherine hurried down the stairs and threw her arms around Justin's neck. "You're just as I remember you—so calm, so matter-of-fact. You greet me as if I've been gone ten days instead of ten years. Does nothing ever surprise you?"

Justin returned her embrace. "I must confess, young lady, that your unexpected visit has caught me a bit by surprise."

"Oh, Justin!" Katherine laughed and hugged him tighter. "I've missed you."

Andi watched the affectionate greeting between her brother and sister and felt a stab of jealousy. Justin was *her* brother—her favorite brother. She wasn't ready to share him with a stranger. She felt worse when she realized that Justin and Katherine had grown up together. It was easy to see they'd been close.

"Andrea," her mother said quietly, "at least say hello to your sister."

Andi narrowed her eyes and glared at the newest family member. *Be polite.* But no words came. She didn't want to say hello to Katherine. She didn't want to say anything to the young woman standing near the wide staircase, except good-bye.

And the sooner, the better, she decided fiercely.

Chapter Six

HOMECOMING

A ndi was spared from having to speak to Katherine by a noisy crash, followed by a shrill cry and the appearance of the same little girl who'd collided with Andi earlier. The youngster raced along the top of the stairs and leaped onto the banister. Sobbing wildly, she flew down the railing and tumbled to the floor at Andi's feet. Then she picked herself up and stared at Andi. Her cries ceased immediately.

"Betsy!" A shout came from the top of the stairs. "Get back here, you—"

Andi gasped at the string of cuss words that spewed from the mouth of the brown-haired boy. She turned to her mother in shock. Elizabeth Carter's lips were pressed tightly together, but she said nothing.

With a loud whoop, the boy threw himself onto the banister railing. Betsy yelped at the sight. She scurried behind Andi and clung tightly to her skirt.

Oh, no! Not again! Andi tried to shake Betsy off. She had no desire to be caught in the middle of another scuffle.

Suddenly, Katherine whipped out a hand and snatched the boy by the arm. "Levi! Shame on you. Hush up and leave your sister alone."

Betsy peeked around Andi's skirt, stuck out her tongue at her brother, and called him a name. A *bad* name.

Andi waited, ears burning, to see what her mother or brother would say about this. To her surprise and outrage, Mother ignored Betsy's outburst.

Justin followed her lead. "Who are these rambunctious, bright-eyed children, Kate?" he asked cheerfully.

Rambunctious? Andi cringed. *More like foul-mouthed brats.*

Katherine smiled weakly and released her grip on the boy. "This is Levi. He's nine."

Levi scowled. "I'm 'most ten."

"Glad to meet you, young man." Justin held out his hand in greeting. "I'm your Uncle Justin." He winked at Andi. "And this young lady who looks just like your mother is your Aunt Andrea. If you want to stay on her good side, however, you'd do well to simply call her Andi."

"We've met," Andi muttered, rubbing her jaw.

Levi shook Justin's hand without speaking. He threw an unfriendly glance in Andi's direction and dismissed her with a shrug.

Katherine sighed. "Say hello, Levi."

"I ain't sayin' hello to no sissy girl."

"I'm sorry," Katherine apologized, red-faced. "It's been a long day." She reached out and drew the little girl from behind Andi. "This is Elizabeth. I named her for Mother."

"I'm Betsy," the child insisted, stamping one small foot. She shoved her mop of unruly brown tangles from her face and stuck out her tongue at Andi.

"But Elizabeth's your real name, sweetie," Katherine said gently. She ignored her daughter's rude gesture.

Melinda spoke up. "Don't forget Hannah. She's adorable," she told Justin. "She's sleeping right now, but wait 'til you see her. I love her already."

"We'll have a chance to get reacquainted tonight," their mother said happily. "Supper's at seven. I'll be in the kitchen if you need anything. Luisa, Nila, and I are preparing your favorite dishes, Katherine." She turned to Andi. "Speaking of supper, I see that it must have been a dusty ride to town. Please change into something suitable for dining.

After all"—she turned a tender look on her oldest daughter—"this is a very special occasion." With that, she swept from the foyer.

Katherine's favorite foods? Andi rolled her eyes. *Something suitable for dining?* She glanced down at her calico. It looked clean to her, and more than fitting for eating supper on a Saturday evening. She threw a helpless look at Melinda, but her sister didn't notice. All her attention was on Justin, Katherine, and the two children.

"You've made Mother happier than I've seen her in a long time, Kate," Justin was saying. "I never realized how much your homecoming would mean to her." He hugged her once more and stepped back. "I think I'll leave you girls to visit, while I catch up on some ranch accounts." He winked at Katherine. "I'm sure Andi and Melinda would love to hear some wild stories from our childhood. You can start with the time you, Chad, and I decided to do a little gold prospecting up in the hills."

A smile twitched at Kate's lips. "Not *that* story, Justin. It's too—"

"I can't," Andi broke in. She knew exactly what Justin was up to, but it wasn't going to work this time. No smooth-talking lawyer tricks would persuade her to spend time with her new sister. "I have to change clothes." Suddenly welcoming the excuse to go to her room, she hurried toward the stairs. "I'll see you all at supper."

She didn't think it was possible to take the stairs *three* at a time, but she did.

Andi would never forget that first supper with Katherine and her children. The table was set as if they were entertaining the governor of California. The silver had been polished until it shone. Everyone was dressed in his or her best. The children were scrubbed, and their hair freshly combed—thanks to Melinda. From the fussing and yelling Andi had overheard, the kids had rarely had a comb taken to their hair, let alone a bath.

While Justin gave a lengthy blessing over the meal, Andi took the opportunity to study her new relatives. None of the children had ever sat at a fancy table before tonight, she decided. It didn't even look like they knew what a prayer was. Betsy was watching everything with wide, brown eyes. Levi stared sullenly at his place setting. Hannah had snatched a biscuit and was stuffing it in her mouth with all the gusto of a starving child.

Justin said, "Amen," but Andi didn't notice. She was too busy following the antics of her nieces and nephew. It wasn't until the platter of roast beef came into her hands that she realized she'd passed everything along without taking a serving. She quickly speared a piece of meat and sent the platter on to Mitch.

Mitch gave her a puzzled look. "All you're having for supper is one slice of roast beef?"

Andi scowled. "All right, so I'll have *two*." She snagged another slice and slapped it on her plate.

Mitch shrugged and took the platter.

Hannah was seated on Melinda's lap, restless and fussy from her late nap. She whined and refused to eat anything but the biscuits, which she shamefully wasted by scattering pieces all over her plate, the tablecloth, and the floor. Halfway through the meal, she suddenly reached out to snatch another biscuit and hit the tumbler of milk that was next to her plate. The liquid splashed onto a serving dish of vegetables and cascaded across the table, drenching the tablecloth.

Like magic, Luisa appeared from the kitchen with some linen napkins to cover the spill. A minute later, she returned with a fresh plate of vegetables and the meal settled into an uncomfortable silence.

"I'm sorry we're spoiling your special dinner, Mother," Katherine said with a catch in her voice. "The children are exhausted, and frankly, we're not used to living like this."

"I understand," Elizabeth assured her daughter. "It's been awhile since we've had little ones at the table." She smiled at her grandchildren. "In a few days, I'm sure you'll be feeling much better."

Betsy yawned and slumped in her chair.

"I asked Nila and her daughter, Rosa, to help with the children for a few days," Elizabeth said. "At least until you're settled in."

Katherine let out a grateful sigh. "Thank you, Mother."

A few minutes later, Rosa and her mother glided into the room. Rosa, smiling and cheerful as ever, helped gather Katherine's children and led them out of the dining room.

"I don't see why I have to go with the baby girls," Levi protested loudly from the doorway. "I ain't sleepy."

"Don't say *ain't,* son," Katherine said wearily. "It's common."

Levi stamped his foot against the hardwood floor. His eyes snapped with challenge. "Well, I *ain't* sleepy and I *ain't* going with those—" His names for Andi's best friend and her mother were less than gracious.

Chad rose from the table and spoke sharply to Levi. "You better get something straight right now, boy. We don't put up with that kind of talk around here. Just do what your mother says, and do it quick."

Levi's mouth dropped open. He turned on his heel and scurried after his sisters, but not before tossing out a parting word for Chad's benefit.

Before Chad could chase after him, Justin raised a hand. "Let it go for now."

Ignore Justin and go after him! Andi wanted to shout. Levi needed a good talking to, but everybody seemed to be passing over his dreadful behavior. She was disappointed and angry when Chad gave Justin a curt nod and resumed his place at the table.

Katherine turned an apologetic look on the rest of the family. "I'm sorry, Mother. Levi just needs to settle in." She bit her lip. "It seems like I've done nothing but apologize since I got here."

"We understand, Katherine. Don't concern yourself."

"Sure," Mitch broke in brightly. "First thing Monday morning I'll get that young cowpoke a mount of his own. Maybe we can wear off some of his energy and bad feelings with a little ranch work."

"Thank you, Mitch."

Elizabeth smiled. "Shall we take coffee and dessert in the parlor?"

"Oh, Mother," Katherine pleaded, "couldn't we stay here? It's been so long since I've sat around the dining room table with my family." A tear trickled down one cheek, quickly followed by another. Soon there was a flood, and she covered her face with her hands and sobbed. Her shoulders shook.

"What's wrong, Katherine?" Elizabeth asked in alarm.

Katherine drew a shaky breath and reached for her napkin. "You've all been so kind. You haven't asked me why I've come home after all these years."

"I think we're afraid to find out," Chad said with his usual bluntness, which drew a warning look from Justin.

"I deserved that," Katherine admitted, wiping her eyes. "But the truth is I'm in trouble. I've nowhere to go, and the children need a safe place to stay."

"Where's Troy?" Chad wanted to know.

Katherine shrugged. "I don't know. I haven't seen him in over a year. His crazy schemes usually kept him away from home for weeks, but he always came back. This time I think he's in trouble with the law and can't come home."

"The law?" Melinda squeaked.

"Yes." Katherine shook her head. "You might as well know. I'm so ashamed. I've made my share of mistakes, but Troy was the biggest mistake of all." She sighed. "He was so handsome, so exciting. Sneaking out to meet him made me feel alive. He always encouraged me and told me how clever I was." Katherine's face crumpled. She suddenly looked old and worn out. It was hard for Andi to believe that her sister was only twenty-five. "Believing Troy's lies was the stupidest thing I ever did. I've paid the price in full, and now I've come home to ask your forgiveness. I only wish Father were here so I could tell him how right he was and how sorry I am." She took a deep breath. "I hope you'll let me stay, at least for a week or two, until I can figure out what I'm going to do."

She looked at Andi. "Mother said she never told you about me. It must be an unpleasant surprise to find out that you have a prodigal for a sister." She shrugged. "My return will no doubt set all the loose tongues in town wagging."

That's for sure, Andi agreed silently. Out loud she said, "Things could be better."

"You should have come home years ago," Justin said. "What took you so long?"

Katherine bowed her head. "I really loved Troy, and I thought he loved me. By the time I found out differently, it was too late. I had a baby to think of." She looked up. Fresh tears glistened at the corners of her eyes. "Troy's nothing but a swindler and a thief. He dragged me all over the country, chasing his ridiculous get-rich-quick schemes. I begged him to let me go home and make things right with my family, but he refused. He told me it was too late; you'd never take me back, not after what I'd done. Troy said I belonged to him now and I'd better not forget it. I was afraid to leave, afraid he'd carry out his threat of hurting me and the children if I ever tried to go home."

The silence around the table grew intense. The coffee turned cold while the family waited to hear the rest of Katherine's story.

Andi swallowed the lump that had suddenly appeared in her throat. She'd heard similar stories before. Sarah Miller's cousin had run away two years ago when the circus passed though town. She'd married one of the acrobats, and what a scandal it had caused. Joey Taylor's brother was caught rustling cattle, along with six others, and had been sent to jail. And of course there was the Hollister clan, shiftless and wild. The oldest girl, Lily, had disappeared last year, only to turn up several months later with a baby in tow. Folks talked about it for weeks. But never had Andi thought such a shameful thing could happen in her own family.

Just wait 'til the kids at school hear about this, she thought. *I won't be able to hold my head up.*

Katherine was still talking. "A couple years ago, Troy disappeared for nearly six months. At first I was glad, for it meant I could settle down and maybe find steady work. Then I discovered he was part of a gang that was robbing stagecoaches. I was afraid—afraid he'd bring his stolen goods home. I wanted no part of that." Katherine started to cry. "Troy did come home. And just as I feared, he brought his share of the loot with him. When I told him I wouldn't touch it, he got ugly. He called me horrible names and stomped out of the house. That was a year ago."

Andi groaned inwardly. *I've got a stagecoach robber for a brother-in-law. This is getting worse and worse.*

Katherine shook her head. "It was bad enough knowing that Troy made a living out of swindling folks, but *this!* I knew I had to get away and start a new life—for my children's sake—before it was too late." She dabbed her eyes with a napkin. "It took me nearly a year to save the money for train fare, and then I worried the entire trip west. What if you didn't want to see me? God knows I don't deserve any sort of welcome for the way I treated you." She shivered and glanced around the table with pleading eyes. "When Troy returns to Chicago and discovers I've left, he'll be furious. He'll hunt me down. Eventually he'll come here. That will put everyone in danger." She paused and drew a deep breath. "If you'll just agree to keep the children, I'll leave and never bother you again."

"That's ridiculous," Justin said. "Of course you'll stay—you and your children—for as long as you like." He pushed back his chair and stood up. "I don't know about the rest of you, but I know what Father would say if he were alive."

Andi watched Justin carefully. What *would* Father have said?

"He'd say, 'Bring the fatted calf, and kill it; and let us eat and be merry. For this my . . . *daughter* . . . was dead, and is alive again; she was lost, and is found.'" Justin opened his arms and smiled. "Welcome home, Kate."

Chapter Seven

RETURN TO THE CREEK

"W hy are you always following me around?" Andi asked her young nephew a week later. She settled the saddle onto Taffy's back and started to cinch it up.

"It's a free country," Levi shot back, laying a hand on the palomino's rump. "Where're you going?"

"Riding."

"Where to?"

"Up to my special spot along the creek." Andi threaded the strap through the ring and gave it a yank. "If that means anything to you."

"It don't. Why're you going there?"

"If you *must* know, I'm taking a few supplies to a poor fellow that Cory, Rosa, and I rescued last week from being buried alive in mud."

Levi's face lit up. "Really? I wanna come."

"You can't."

"Why not?"

Andi lost her temper. "Because I'm tired of you tagging behind me wherever I go!" She didn't dare tell Levi the real reason—that she didn't trust him not to blab about T. J. to the rest of the family.

Andi had managed to slip away to the creek earlier in the week, with a grub sack and a canteen for the unfortunate stranger. She'd even managed to snag him a wide-brimmed hat to keep the sun off his head. T. J. had been pleased to see her and said so. Andi figured one more supply trip would be enough to assure herself the handsome young stranger could fend for himself.

Levi gave Andi a scheming look. "If you don't let me go, I'll tell Grandmother what you're up to."

"You better not!"

"Then take me with you. I can ride. Uncle Mitch gave me Patches for my very own."

Andi bit back the angry reply that leaped to her lips. *You don't deserve a pony.*

Mitch's gift to Levi annoyed her, as did all the attention her brother was heaping on their horrid little nephew. He'd spent hours teaching Levi to ride, and boasted to anyone who would listen what a good rider the boy was. What's more, he'd redone Levi's chores all week. When Andi pointed out that Levi should do his own chores, Mitch had grinned and said, "I've done *your* chores plenty of times, sis. Why shouldn't I lend a hand to Levi?" There was truth in her brother's words, but it irritated Andi all the same.

With a scowl at the memory, Andi finished saddling Taffy. "You can't come," she told Levi. She dropped the stirrup in place, grabbed the reins, and pulled herself into the saddle. "You can go with me another time," she relented, seeing the hurt look on Levi's face. "I'm in a hurry today."

Indeed, if she wanted to make it to the creek and back before the October sun set, she'd have to hustle. There was never enough time to ride after school, and the shorter fall days cut deeply into this pleasure. Without waiting for a response from Levi, she urged Taffy into a lope and headed for the hills.

Free at last! Andi rejoiced at the few minutes of peace and privacy she planned to enjoy on her ride up to her special spot. It had been a dreadful week, and watching Mitch and Levi together was only a small part of it. Adjusting to new family members was a lesson Andi wasn't learning well. It had taken her only a few days to realize that having her oldest sister—and especially the three children—on the ranch would be the biggest challenge of her life.

Her cheeks burned when she recalled Justin's tongue-lashing from the day before. She'd been in a particularly sour mood on the ride home from school and had poured out her complaints without thinking.

"It's 'Katherine this' and 'Katherine that.'" Andi had crossed her arms and slouched against the back of the buggy. "'Would you like to go riding this afternoon, Katherine?'" She mimicked her mother's gentle voice. "'Diego can saddle Snowflake for you, Katherine. I'll have him saddle Champ for me.' 'Katherine, shall we go into town today and visit the dressmaker? She has some lovely silks just in from San Francisco.'" Andi clenched her teeth in frustration. "Every time I try to talk to Mother, she has one of those whiny little girls on her lap. I can't finish a sentence without being interrupted. Worse, they follow me around wherever I go. And Levi! He's awful! If you only heard the name he called me yesterday—"

"That will be about enough from you."

If Justin had slapped her, Andi would not have been more surprised. She jerked her head around and stared at her brother, speechless.

"I know you've been out of sorts lately," Justin continued, "and I don't blame you. You were hurt to find out about Katherine so suddenly. I'm sorry. That's our fault. However"—he fixed a stern look on her—"it's over. Katherine is your sister, and she'll be staying at the ranch for as long as she needs to. So will the children. You will stop this petty complaining and try to be a little understanding. Do I make myself clear?"

Andi had nodded and kept quiet the rest of the way home.

Even now, on her way to the creek, Justin's scolding cast a shadow over her pleasant ride. Her stomach clenched. She scowled, shook herself free of her musing, and urged Taffy into a gallop.

Half an hour later, she topped a small rise and came into view of her favorite spot on the ranch. She grinned at the sight of T. J. Silver lifting his arm in welcome. He was standing with his large bay gelding, next to what was left of the creek. When Andi drew near, he called out a greeting.

"Howdy yourself," Andi shouted back. She reined Taffy to a stop and dismounted. "Look at you! You're up and around—good as new."

T. J. removed his hat and bowed. "Thanks to you, I feel like a new man. All those hearty sandwiches and a chance to rest without worrying about being chased down did the trick." He smiled. "Seriously, Andi, I don't know how I can ever repay you. You and your friends most likely saved my life the other day."

His gratitude warmed Andi clear through. "You don't have to repay me. I was happy to help." She reached out and tugged at the sack of food tied to her saddle horn. "I'm sure you'd do the same for me," she added, handing over the supplies.

T. J. took the grub sack and tossed it to the ground. "Hard to say. Where I come from, folks aren't so quick to lend a hand. Too many ruffians around to rob 'em when their backs are turned."

Andi paused and took a long, hard look at her new friend. She sure hoped *he* wasn't one of those ruffians he was talking about. He certainly looked the part, though, with his wild hair and the scraggly new growth on his face. It suddenly dawned on her that Cory was right. She knew nothing about Mr. T. J. Silver. "Where are you from?" she asked abruptly. "And what are you doing here?"

He ran his fingers through his light brown tangles and replaced his hat. For a moment, his eyes darkened. "Where I come from, folks also don't ask a lot of pesky questions." Then his eyes turned merry and he chuckled. "Don't worry, Andi. I'm not going to rob you. Where am I from? East of the Mississippi. What am I doing here? Looking for work. Know any spreads needing an extra hand?"

Andi smiled in relief. "Sure! Our ranch. There're always fences to mend or posts to be cut. I'm sure Sid could find you work, at least until you're ready to—"

"Say, Andi. Who's your friend?"

Andi turned and shaded her eyes. A small figure on a sharp-looking pinto pony was galloping over the rise. Levi! He must have followed her. Andi groaned. "It's my nephew. He won't leave me alone."

T. J. pulled his hat over his forehead, folded his arms across his chest, and grinned. "Nephew? You don't look old enough to be an aunt."

Andi cringed. She hated being called aunt. Furious with Levi for invading her privacy, she took off running to meet him. "Don't bother to dismount," she called as he pulled up beside her. "Just hightail it back to the ranch this minute."

Levi tossed the reins aside and slid off his pony. "You're not my boss." He pointed at T. J., who was bent over, checking his horse's feet. "Is that the poor fella you rescued?"

"Never mind," Andi snapped. "You get back on that pony and go home." She was seething. Levi had followed her to her special place!

Levi took two steps toward T. J., but Andi caught his shirtsleeve. "You mount up and get back to the ranch or I'll tell Chad you're not taking proper care of Patches. You might have Mitch wrapped around your little finger, but you can't fool Chad."

Andi's words stopped Levi in his tracks. It was obvious he preferred to steer clear of his tall, short-tempered uncle. They both knew Chad had no patience with sloppy or unfinished chores. Levi shot her a look of pure hatred and jerked away from her grasp. But he climbed onto his pony. "All right. I'm leaving. But you've got to come too."

Disgusted, Andi returned to the creek and grabbed Taffy's reins. "I'd better head back," she told T. J., "before somebody wonders what happened to Levi."

T. J. straightened up and nodded. "Thanks for the supplies. This should get me by a couple more days. Then I'll check with that fore-man of yours . . . Sid?"

"Sid McCoy," Andi said, mounting her horse.

"Much obliged. I'll see you around." He waved and returned to his careful examination of his horse.

Andi nudged Taffy and called to Levi. "Let's get going. If somebody comes looking for us, we'll both be in trouble."

With a shrug of apparent indifference, Levi gathered up the reins. He turned a sly look on Andi and smirked. "Whenever you're ready, *Auntie* Andi."

Chapter Eight

A HANDFUL OF NIECES

A ndi fumed silently most of the way back to the ranch. *Auntie Andi indeed!* She knew Levi called her that just to annoy her—and it worked every time. She glanced behind her to make sure he was keeping up.

"Wanna race?" he asked when he caught her look.

As much as she wanted to refuse, she couldn't pass up an invitation to race. She waited until Levi was beside her and then gave a curt nod.

With an ear-splitting Indian war cry, the boy slammed his heels into his pinto pony and took off like a shot. Andi gulped back her surprise, tightened her hold on the reins, and urged Taffy into a gallop. Catching Levi would be a challenge. He rode as if a pack of hungry wolves were after him. He clung to his horse like a burr, shouting his encouragement and shrieking with laughter. It was nothing short of amazing, considering Levi's first ride on a horse had occurred less than a week ago. Mitch had boasted how quickly Levi had taken to riding; now Andi could see it for herself.

"Nice race," she admitted when they were cooling down their mounts. She hadn't realized the pinto was so fast. With Levi's head start, she'd been hard-pressed to catch up. She'd barely managed to end the race with a tie.

"Next time I'm gonna beat you," Levi bragged.

"You can try," Andi said with a sudden grin.

Levi grunted his opinion of that, but surprised Andi by returning the grin. His earlier anger at her seemed to have dissolved. Together, they turned into the yard and dismounted. Levi dutifully led Patches into the stall Mitch had readied for him.

Andi entered Taffy's stall to rub down her horse. Her eyes widened to find Betsy crouched in a corner.

"I been waiting for hours and hours, Andi," the little girl said in an exasperated voice.

"What for?"

Betsy scrambled to her feet. "For you. I wanna help." She snatched up a brush, scurried beneath Taffy, and began attacking the mare's underbelly with quick, careless strokes. Taffy quivered and flicked her ears.

"Get out from under there, before you get stepped on."

Betsy crawled out and stood up. "I wanna help."

Andi sighed. "All right." She took the brush from Betsy and showed her how to groom the mare properly. Less than five minutes later, the little girl was under Taffy again, brushing her belly and poking at her.

"Betsy, I told you to stay out from under there."

Betsy tossed the brush to the ground and made her way to the back of the stall. "I'm going to braid her tail." Grabbing two fistfuls of the stiff, cream-colored hair, Betsy yanked.

Taffy tossed her head, shied away, and slammed into Andi, pinning her against the side of the stall.

Andi gasped at the crushing pain. Tears sprang to her eyes. She slapped her horse angrily and spoke between clenched teeth. "Move over." Wriggling away from the huge golden body, she clutched her aching ribs and rounded on Betsy. "Get away from my horse." She longed to sink down into the hay and catch her breath, but Taffy was growing more agitated by the minute. Andi knew it wouldn't be long before her horse lost all patience with the small nuisance hanging on her tail.

Betsy's eyes welled up with tears. "I wanna make Taffy look pretty."

"You're going to get us both hurt. Now get on out of here . . .
now!"

Betsy didn't move. Andi reached for her, but Betsy scuttled out of
the way, still clutching Taffy's tail.

Taffy whinnied and shook her mane. She laid her ears back and
danced nervously.

Andi caught Betsy and yanked her away just as Taffy lashed out
with a hind foot. It narrowly missed the girls and landed with a
crash against the stall's back wall. The sound of splintering wood
filled the air.

"Now see what you've done!" With one hand firmly gripping Betsy's
wrist, Andi dragged her across the stall. With her other hand, she
fumbled for the latch until it slipped aside. Then she shoved the stall's
half-door open and pushed Betsy through the opening. The little girl
tripped and landed in the aisle. "Get out and stay out."

Betsy scrambled to her feet and rubbed her grubby fists in her eyes.
She stamped her foot and burst into fresh tears. "I'm gonna tell my
mama on you! You're mean and stupid! Your horse stinks!" Her voice
rose until her words gave way to high-pitched screeching. Each shriek
was accompanied by a desperate kick in Andi's direction.

"Hey!" Andi skipped out of the way. She ducked into Taffy's stall
and slammed the door shut. Betsy pounded on the half-door and
screamed.

"What's all the commotion in here?" Chad shouted over the noise.
He made his way to Taffy's stall, saw Betsy beating her fists against
the door, and looked at his sister. "Good grief, Andi, what did you
do to her? We can hear her screeching clear across the yard."

"I told her to leave. That's all. She nearly got kicked." Andi had
to holler to be heard.

Chad turned his attention to Betsy. "Stop that howling and go
find your mother."

Betsy shrank visibly at Chad's rebuke, gulped back a sob, and scampered out of the barn.

Andi rested her arms across the half-door and gave her brother a grateful smile. "Thanks for the help."

"My pleasure." He let out a disgusted breath. "I don't know why Kate doesn't make those kids mind. They're wild little things. Half the time they're bold as brass, and the rest of the time they act scared of their own shadows." He gave Andi an understanding look. "I know you're having trouble adjusting to Kate's return. If you need to get off by yourself for a little peace and quiet sometime, let me know. I'll find something for you to do away from the house."

"Thanks. I'll remember that." Andi hung over the door for a few minutes, watching her brother leave; then, with a sigh of relief, she returned to her chores. She glanced at the gaping hole in the wall and bit her lip. "Good thing Chad didn't see this," she murmured, giving Taffy a pat. "Maybe I can get one of the hands to fix it before he finds out."

With that decided, Andi gently combed out Taffy's tail, apologizing for the rough treatment the mare had received. "I wish I could stay longer, but it's getting late. I've got to get back inside and help with supper." She gave Taffy a hug, dumped a measure of oats into her feeder, and left. It wasn't hard to find a sympathetic ranch hand to mend Taffy's stall, and Andi felt relieved as she headed for the house.

Mother was waiting for her when Andi entered the kitchen. "What happened in the barn, Andrea? Betsy ran into the house, screaming at the top of her lungs."

Andi crossed to the sink and shoved her hands under the kitchen pump. She grabbed the soap and said, "She pulled Taffy's tail and got me smashed against the stall. Then Chad came in and told her to go find her mother." Andi dried her hands and looked around. "Where is she?"

"Upstairs with Katherine. She's washing her up and trying to calm her. You didn't hit Betsy, did you?"

"Of course not. But I did drag her out of Taffy's stall. I wasn't gentle about it, either." She tossed the towel aside. "And I guess I yelled at her too. I'm sorry."

Her mother gave her an understanding look. "I know this has been hard for you, sweetheart. It takes some getting used to, having younger children around the house."

Andi remembered Justin's warning and bit off a quick retort before it could find its way out of her mouth. "I know," she agreed. "I just wish . . ."

"What do you wish?"

"The honest truth?"

Her mother nodded.

"Everything's turned upside down since Katherine's come home," she confessed. "I wish she . . . she . . ." Andi fumbled for words.

"You wish she'd never come home?" her mother finished for her.

Andi dropped her gaze and nodded. She felt her face grow hot.

Elizabeth reached out and pulled Andi into a tender hug. "I know Katherine must seem like a complete stranger to you. Please try to remember that she was once a little girl like you, and I love her as much as I love you. I want her to feel comfortable staying on the ranch for as long as she wants—until things settle down for her and the children. Can you be patient?"

"I don't know." Andi unwound her arms from around her mother's waist. "But I'll try," she promised.

Andi's noble intention to show patience toward her sister's family dissolved the instant she entered her bedroom to change clothes. She stifled a scream at the sight before her. The room looked as if an earthquake had struck. The bed was rumpled and unmade. Dirty footprints danced across the quilt and onto the floor. A shelf containing her collection of favorite books was empty, the books scattered across the room like jackstraws.

With a low moan, Andi explored the devastation. The top of her bureau was strewn with the contents of her treasure box. Marbles, a small gold nugget, a seashell, a miniature portrait of her mother and father, and other precious items were scattered and damaged.

She picked up an eagle's feather—a gift from an Indian boy she'd met riding one day years ago. She'd been eight years old and scared to death at the sight of the tall, bronze youth on his horse. Indian savagery had been an exciting, ongoing subject at school in those days. But the young brave had smiled at her and had given her the feather. She'd offered him a hair ribbon. Both had ridden away content, with not one word passing between them.

The eagle's feather now looked as if someone had chewed on it. She tried to smooth the individual lengths back in place, but the damage was done.

Andi found her treasure box upside down on the floor next to the bureau. She scooped it up with one hand and carefully laid the feather inside. Then she gathered up the rest of her collection, pausing a moment to shake the huge rattle from the snake Mitch had killed up in the hills last summer. He'd brought the rattle home just for her, claiming it was the largest snake he'd ever seen. Thankfully, the delicate scales of the rattle appeared undamaged. She set it next to the feather.

As she gathered up the remainder of her treasures—the gold nugget, a dozen agate marbles, a bullet Cory Blake insisted came from the leg of an old Yankee soldier he'd met—Andi's anger burned hot and quick. Who would dare rummage through her things? Who would enter her bedroom without permission?

"I bet it was Levi," she decided wrathfully, rolling up the dirty quilt and dropping it onto the floor. "I'll pay him back for this. I really will." Then she paused. When would Levi have had time to wreck her room? She knew Mitch was keeping him busy around the ranch.

"Hi, Nandi," a tiny voice piped up.

Andi spun around. In the doorway stood Hannah, her golden curls sticking up everywhere, her face flushed from sleep. She was clutching a battered rag doll. Around the doll's neck hung a locket—the locket Justin had given Andi for her twelfth birthday last spring.

Andi caught her breath in sudden realization. Hannah had destroyed her room! Only a three-year-old could have torn things up so completely and jumped on her bed with such abandon. Hannah would think nothing of tasting an eagle's feather or dumping out a box and then tossing it to the floor in boredom.

"See my pretty dolly." Hannah held up her doll for Andi to see. She popped her thumb in her mouth and waited for Andi's response.

Andi exploded. "Give me my locket!"

Hannah's cornflower blue eyes filled with tears. She removed her thumb and set up a wail. "*My* lecklace," she insisted loudly, grasping the locket with a chubby hand. "Mine."

Andi took a step toward her little niece. "It's *not* yours. It's mine, and you took it. You also destroyed my room and got into my things."

Hannah turned tail and ran. She rushed to the top of the stairs, sobbing. Andi followed and snatched her up before the tiny girl could tumble down the stairs. She tucked Hannah under her arm and sailed down the staircase.

"Mother!" She stormed into the kitchen, a howling Hannah still under her arm.

Melinda, with a now-quiet Betsy sitting beside her at the table, looked up in surprise.

Katherine rushed over. "What happened?" She pulled Hannah from Andi's arms. "Shh, darling. It's all right. Did you wake up frightened from your nap?"

Hannah sobbed and clutched her mother. "Mine!"

"Andrea?" Mother raised her eyebrows in confusion. "Do you know why she's carrying on?"

"You bet I do. Hannah tore my room apart, jumped all over my bed with her dirty feet, and took the locket Justin gave me."

"How could she have done that?" Katherine asked. "She's been asleep."

"I guess she wasn't as asleep as you thought," Andi snapped. She reached for Hannah's doll. Hannah shrieked.

Katherine sat down and cradled Hannah in her lap. "Let me see Tessie, sweetie." The little girl tearfully held out the doll for her mother's inspection. Katherine's face reddened at the sight of the locket. She carefully removed it and dropped it into Andi's waiting hands. "I'm sorry, Andi. I put her to bed right after the noon meal. She must have gotten up and done some exploring before going to sleep." She bit her lip. "Is there much damage?"

Andi's anger cooled somewhat at her sister's apology. She fastened the locket securely around her neck and shook her head. "Things are mostly scattered all over the place. Nothing that can't be fixed, I guess. The quilt will have to be washed. Her footprints are all over it."

Katherine lifted Hannah's chin. "You've been very naughty, Hannah. You mustn't go into Andi's room."

Hannah stared into her mother's eyes. She turned and looked forlornly at the empty neck of her doll. Then she glanced at Andi. Her lower lip quivered. "*My* lecklace," she whimpered, reaching for the locket hanging around Andi's neck.

"No, Hannah. It's Andi's necklace. You must tell her you're sorry."

Hannah put her thumb in her mouth and looked down into her mother's lap. She shook her head. When Katherine attempted to remove her small daughter's thumb, she howled.

"Katherine," Andi began uncomfortably. "It's all right." She suddenly felt like a scoundrel for making Hannah unhappy. "Could you please just keep her out of my room?"

Katherine nodded. "I'll watch Hannah more closely. Would you like me to go up and straighten your room?"

Andi was strangely moved by her sister's humble words. "No. I'll clean it myself. You don't know where anything goes." She smiled at Katherine. "Thanks just the same."

"Andi?" Betsy jumped up and took hold of Andi's hand. "Can I help you? Please? I'm sorry I pulled Taffy's tail and said mean things to you."

Andi glanced down into Betsy's pleading brown eyes. She felt the little girl's small, warm hand clasping hers in eagerness. "All right. You can help me. And if you do a good job and promise to mind me when we're around Taffy, I'll let you look inside my secret box."

"A truly secret box?" Betsy's eyes grew wide.

Andi grinned at the awe on Betsy's face. She nodded. "Say, Betsy, have you ever shaken a rattlesnake's rattle?"

Betsy shook her head, dumbfounded. "Will it bite?"

Andi couldn't help it. She laughed. "No, silly. It's the rattle of the snake, not the mouth." She gave Betsy a tug. "Come on."

Betsy beamed her delight. She squeezed Andi's hand and whispered, "I like you, Andi. I really, really do."

Andi felt the hard shell around her heart crack—just a little.

Chapter Nine

TROUBLE IN THE SCHOOLYARD

This is my nephew, Levi Swanson," Andi announced at school the following Monday. Katherine had decided that Levi had adjusted to the ranch, and it was time to settle into school for the final weeks before the holidays. Neither Andi nor Levi received the news with joy. "He's staying out at the ranch for a while," she explained to Levi's teacher.

There were a few muffled giggles at this. Andi pressed her lips tightly together. Everybody in Fresno—including the schoolchildren—knew who was staying at the Circle C and why. It hadn't taken long for word to spread about the mysterious return of a long-lost sister of questionable reputation. It made for great gossip around town. Andi especially dreaded Sunday mornings, when the folks at church spent more time staring at her family and whispering than listening to the preacher.

"Welcome, Levi," Miss Hall said cheerfully. "How old are you?"

"Almost ten."

Miss Hall recorded his name and age in the roll book and glanced up. "Now, where shall I seat you?"

Toby Wright waved an eager hand in the air. "He can sit with me, Miss Hall. Frankie took sick last week and won't be back before the holidays."

"Fine. Have you any books, Levi?"

"Yes'm. My aunt gave me some of her old ones." The class tittered. "What's so funny?" he demanded. "Andi *is* my aunt, so there!"

"That's true, Levi. And you couldn't have a nicer one." Miss Hall smiled at Andi until Andi felt squirmy all over. Being called "aunt" was disgusting, and Levi only did it to pester her.

"Thank you, Auntie Andi, for helping me find my class." The look in Levi's eyes mocked her.

The class howled with laughter. Levi smirked.

"Just see if I help you with anything else," Andi whispered furiously in Levi's ear. "Now go sit down and don't give Miss Hall any trouble."

Levi responded by shoving Andi aside and stomping off to his new seat beside Toby.

As Andi left the classroom, she heard Toby chattering away. "You're lucky to have Andi for an aunt, Levi. She's the nicest girl in the whole school, and she plays ball near as good as the big boys. I wish she was *my* aunt."

Levi grunted a reply, which sounded like, "You can have her."

Andi shook her head and headed for the stairs that led up to her classroom, deep in thought. She wished there were something she could find to like in her ornery, smart-mouthed nephew. He seemed to despise her, yet he followed her around from dawn 'til dusk. He was an ill-mannered little brat, foul-mouthed and ready to start a fight over the smallest offense. He made it clear that he had no use for sissy girls—especially Andi. He never talked about his father. The only person he appeared to respect and truly like was Mitch.

"You could have told me Katherine Swanson is your sister." The words yanked Andi from her thoughts. She looked up. Cory was blocking her way. He crossed his arms over his chest and gave her a hurt look. "That day in town, remember? You could have told me. Instead, I had to find out from the town busybodies." He dropped his arms to his sides. "I thought we were friends."

Andi didn't know what to say. She'd been so caught up in her own misery the past couple of weeks that she'd hardly noticed Cory, much less talked to him at school. She turned away.

Cory wasn't finished with her. "And another thing. What about that suspicious-looking fella up at the creek? I suppose you took him supplies? By yourself, I bet."

Andi whirled. "So what if I did? T. J.'s not suspicious-looking. He's friendly, and very grateful for our help. I told him to ask Sid for a job."

Cory rolled his eyes, but before he could comment, the bell rang. He and Andi exchanged a look of panic and clattered up the steps, forgetting their disagreement for the time being.

"Miss Carter. Mr. Blake." The schoolmaster pierced them with a look when they rushed into the classroom. "The tardy bell has found you out of your seats."

"I'm sorry, Mr. Foster." Andi slid quickly into the double seat she shared with Rosa. "I had to show my nephew his class and introduce him to his teacher. I didn't mean for it to take so long."

"And your excuse, Mr. Blake?"

Cory gave the teacher an innocent smile. "I was seeing Miss Carter safely up the stairs."

There were a few snickers, which Mr. Foster cut short. "I see." He kept his face a mask, but his eyes showed his amusement. "I will suspend the consequences for being tardy this time, because you were assisting a new student. But tomorrow . . ." He let the unspoken warning hang in the air.

"Yes, sir," Andi and Cory replied together.

"Andi!" someone shouted during recess. "Come quick!"

Andi froze. The jump rope slapped against her ankles and sent her to the ground with an unladylike *thud*. "Ouch!"

"*Lo siento*," Rosa apologized, dropping the rope. "It happened so fast."

"It's all right." She rose and dusted off her skirt.

"Andi!" The shout came again, this time accompanied by the sounds of a scuffle.

Toby Wright ran up and grabbed her hand. His eyes were wide with alarm. "Hurry! Levi's fighting Jacob Powers."

"Oh, no!" Andi raced after Toby and found the two boys rolling in the dust. Right behind her, Miss Hall made an appearance. They were just in time to hear Levi swear soundly at Jacob and call him a name that made Andi flush in anger and embarrassment. "Levi! Jacob! Stop it!" she shouted.

The boys ignored her. Jacob was hollering and thrashing and sobbing, but Levi refused to back off. His fist crashed into Jacob's red face.

Fear gripped Andi. Quiet, sensitive Jacob was no match for Levi. He was the only child of Matthew Powers, an attorney in town and Justin's friend and colleague. Mr. Powers set great store by his small son and would certainly take offense at Levi's attack. How in the world had Levi gotten himself into such a fix?

Andi didn't stand still wondering for long. She took a deep breath and waded into the scuffle. To her surprise and relief, Cory joined her. He rescued Jacob from under Levi, leaving the bigger boy to Andi. She gripped him by his shoulders and gave a yank that sent him sprawling. "Levi! Stop it!"

Levi leaped up and threw himself at Jacob again. Cory backed away, pulling Jacob with him. He deflected Levi's blow with his free arm and pushed him aside. "Quite the nephew you've got, Andi. A real wildcat."

Andi ignored Cory and reached for Levi, who was shouting at Jacob, "Come back here, you little—"

Just in time, Andi clapped her hand over Levi's mouth. He responded by slamming an elbow into her stomach and prying her hand away. "Let me go. It's my fight."

Andi didn't let go. She didn't dare. She set her jaw, ignored the pain in her belly, and hung onto Levi as a curious crowd gathered around them.

By the time Mr. Foster arrived, things had settled down. The schoolmaster frowned at Levi. "You, sir, will explain the meaning of this."

Levi shook himself free of Andi's grip and wiped a sleeve across his bloody nose. "That low-down, stinkin—" He caught himself, saw Andi glaring at him, and bit his lip. "That sniveling baby accused me of swiping his marbles. I didn't."

"You *did* steal them," a soft voice piped up. Jacob stood quietly by Cory, a handkerchief to his nose. Both eyes were already turning black and blue. His shirt was torn, and a thick coat of dust covered his britches. "If you look in his pocket, you'll find my best aggie and two steelies. I want 'em back."

Andi thrust her fingers into the pocket of Levi's overalls. He stood as still as a statue, watching her. She withdrew her hand and uncurled her fingers. Three shiny marbles gleamed up from her palm. She lifted the marbles to Levi's face. "What are these, Levi?"

"I won 'em. Fair and square. But this baby boy is too stingy to admit it."

"That's not true, Andi," Jacob said. "Ask Toby. Ask anybody. When my back was turned, Levi snatched the marbles from the circle and ran off."

Levi turned to Andi. "I did not!" His lip quivered. "It's because I'm new here. It always happens. Nobody ever believes me. They all gang up on me and make fun of me, just 'cause I don't have no pa." Two large tears fell from his eyes.

There was a sudden, sympathetic murmur from Miss Hall. "Poor little thing."

Andi glanced past Levi and saw Toby shaking his head. Frowning, she stepped away from her nephew. "Don't waste your tears on me, Levi. You took the marbles." She was so angry and confused that she wanted to slap him. Instead, she clutched the marbles until they dug into her palm. "Didn't you?"

Levi's wounded look turned sullen. "So what if I did?"

Andi turned her back on Levi and walked stiffly over to Jacob. "Here're your marbles, Jacob. I'm sorry Levi took them. I'm sure his mother will speak to him about it."

But Andi *wasn't* sure. She'd discovered early on that Katherine seemed afraid to discipline her children. Whether she felt sorry for them, or whether she didn't know how to handle their misbehavior, Andi couldn't tell.

Mr. Foster clearly had no such misgivings. He turned to Miss Hall. "With your permission, ma'am, I will thrash this unruly young pupil of yours, in order to teach him not to lie and steal and fight."

Miss Hall looked at Levi and shook her head. "Not today, Mr. Foster, although I appreciate your offer. If it happens again, I will certainly call on your services. I think for now we will temper justice with mercy for Levi's first day of school." Her look turned stern. "I insist, however, that you apologize to Jacob."

Levi stuck out his lower lip and muttered a clipped apology. Then he shuffled back to the schoolhouse, head bowed.

Jacob sniffed back a few tears and looked at Andi. "When Papa sees my face, he's going to be mighty upset. He'll want to know how it happened."

Andi watched Levi enter the schoolhouse. "I reckon."

"I'll have to tell him." Jacob sounded regretful.

"I guess your father will be calling on my sister."

"Yep," Jacob said softly. Then he hurried away to join his friends.

Andi felt drained. She started back to class, too tired to return to her rope jumping. What would her mother say when she found out about Levi's fight? Would she wonder why Andi hadn't prevented such a scene? "Probably," she muttered, kicking a rock. Somehow, she knew Levi's troubles would soon become her own.

Chapter Ten

MORE TROUBLE

A ndi and Levi crouched side by side on the second-story landing. They pressed their faces against the balcony railing and
struggled to hear the conversation coming from the parlor below
them and out of sight.

"Jacob's pa looked all fired up when Grandmother invited him
in," Levi whispered. "Do you suppose Mama will ask Uncle Justin
to whip me?"

Andi hesitated before answering. "I . . . I . . . don't know. Justin's
real patient most times, but I suppose if Mr. Powers insists, he'll probably have to do it. After all, you pounded Jacob pretty good."

Levi cringed and squeezed his eyes shut. Tears oozed between his
eyelids and trickled down his cheeks.

Andi reached out and laid a gentle hand on his shoulder. Suddenly,
he didn't seem so much a pest, only a scared little boy. She couldn't
help feeling sorry for him. She knew what it felt like to be worried
about a whipping. "Maybe your mother will do it herself."

Levi shook his head and brushed a hand across his cheek. "She
won't. She never does. I guess she figures Pa thrashed me enough for
the both of 'em. I got it nearly every day when he was home."

Andi swallowed her uneasiness at Levi's words. Against her will,
she whispered, "Why?"

Levi glanced up. "Why what?"

"Why did your father whip you every day?"

"That's Pa," he replied, as if it made perfect sense. "Lots of things riled him." He shrugged. "'Specially when he had too much to drink."

"But—"

"Hush!" Levi nudged her impatiently. "Don't you want to hear what they're saying?"

The two returned to their eavesdropping. Andi glanced at Levi from the corner of her eye. Her heart thumped against the inside of her chest as she considered his words. Thrashed every day? No wonder he was afraid of getting a whipping. She bit her lip and wondered how Levi had come to deserve such a fate. Sure, he was a pest, but . . . *every day?* Andi shuddered.

"Hey! What're you doing?" Betsy's piping voice shattered the silence—and Andi's thoughts.

"Shhh!" Levi reached out and pulled his sister to the floor. "You've got a mouth like a hippopotamus."

Betsy responded with a shriek that pierced Andi's and Levi's ears. "Let me go, or I'll tell Mama you're spying on—"

Andi clapped a frantic hand over the little girl's mouth, but it was too late.

"What is going on up there?" Elizabeth Carter strolled into the foyer and looked up at the landing. Behind her, Katherine and Mr. Powers waited. "Andrea, I asked you a question. Please come down."

Andi threw a disgusted look at Betsy and slowly made her way down the stairs. The two younger children followed in silence.

When all three stood before her, Elizabeth nodded. "I'm waiting."

"I'm sorry, Mother," Andi said. "We wanted to hear what Mr. Powers and Kate were talking about."

"Fine. You might as well hear what will happen to Levi. Katherine?"

Katherine stepped forward and looked sorrowfully at her son.

"What you did was wrong, Levi—very wrong. You returned the marbles, but the injury you caused Jacob cannot be overlooked. I assured Mr. Powers that you will be punished with the switch for hurting his son."

Levi made a sound like a frightened puppy and clutched Andi's sleeve. Andi didn't shake him off like she normally would have.

Katherine's blue eyes filled with tears at her son's hopeless expression. "Oh, Levi! How could you cause me such sorrow?" She bowed her head. Her thin shoulders shook with quiet sobs.

Levi found his voice. "Don't cry, Mama. It wasn't my fault. Honest."

"Levi," Katherine warned between sobs, "don't add lying to your—"

"Levi's right," Andi said.

Everyone turned to her in surprise.

"How's that, young lady?" Mr. Powers asked. He folded his arms across his chest and silently demanded an explanation.

"It's—it's *my* fault," Andi said. Levi gawked at her. "It was Levi's first day of school. I should've watched out for him, showed him around, and told him the rules. If I'd been with him, he wouldn't have stolen Jacob's marbles, which would have kept him out of the fight. I'll watch him better from now on, if you'll let him off from getting whipped." She straightened her shoulders and looked at Mr. Powers. "If you insist on punishing someone, Mr. Powers, you can ask Justin to . . . to . . ." She paused. "Well, you can ask him to whip *me*."

Elizabeth stared at her daughter as if seeing her for the first time. Her face showed her surprise, but she said nothing.

"I see," Mr. Powers said. He rubbed his cheek, frowned slightly, and took a deep breath. "A very interesting offer, young lady. Are you just saying words, or do you mean it?"

"I mean it. I know Levi's a lot of trouble, but it was his first day of school among strangers."

Mr. Powers held Andi's steady blue gaze for a full minute. Then he sighed. "Very well. I'll leave this matter in Justin's hands, so long as that boy"—he shot an irritated glance at Levi—"stays far away from my son. Is that understood?"

"Yes, sir," Andi agreed.

Mr. Powers nodded curtly. "You've got yourself quite a job." With a grunt, he turned sharply on his heel and headed toward the door. Opening it, he paused. "Good day, Mrs. Carter. Thank you for your time."

The door closed. Everyone let out a sigh of relief. Katherine sank into a nearby chair and let her tears flow once more.

"Aw, Mama," Levi burst out, "don't start crying again. I'll leave that stupid ol' Jacob Powers alone."

"Indeed you will, young man," Elizabeth said. "But for now, you will march out to the woodpile and bring in a full load of wood for the box in the kitchen. Later, when your Uncle Mitch comes in from the range, you'll do whatever chores he assigns you—without a word of complaint."

Levi gaped at his grandmother. "But . . ." His voice trailed off at the expression on her face. He looked at Katherine. "Mama?" His mother shook her head and said nothing.

"March," Elizabeth ordered briskly. Levi took off running toward the kitchen.

Andi hid a pleased smile behind her hand. So far, her mother had been unusually patient and loving toward Levi. She had put up with his sassy mouth and stomping feet without a word, much to Andi's surprise and outrage. She wouldn't dare talk to her mother the way Levi did. This sudden change of attitude in his grandmother seemed to frighten Levi, and Andi was glad. Somebody had to make Levi mind, and Katherine didn't appear up to the task.

"Forgive me for interfering, Katherine," Elizabeth said, "but I'm afraid I can no longer allow Levi to misbehave. I tried to give him time to settle in, but his attitude is affecting the entire household."

Katherine shook her head. "You needn't apologize, Mother. I'm embarrassed to admit how dreadful Levi behaves. I never noticed, not until we arrived here. I had so many things on my mind—like surviving and getting away from Troy—that raising my children was set aside."

Elizabeth nodded. "I understand, dear." She turned to Andi. "Andrea, you certainly silenced Mr. Powers with your surprising offer. I'm proud of you."

Andi bit her lip. It had felt good at the time to help Levi out of a tight spot, especially since she believed she was partly to blame for the boy's trouble; but she didn't feel so good now. "Is Justin going to . . . ?" She swallowed and looked at her mother.

Elizabeth drew Andi into a warm embrace. "Not if I have anything to say about it. Mr. Powers left the decision in Justin's hands, but I'm sure your brother will agree that the matter is settled."

Katherine stood up. "Andi, I'd like to speak with you. Do you think you could join me in the library?" She paused. "Please?"

Andi hesitated and narrowed her eyes. Up until now, she'd avoided spending much time alone with Katherine. Three weeks had not yet melted all the resentment she still harbored against her sister's unexpected return. True, Andi had begun to accept and even feel a little warmth toward the children, especially Betsy, but she wasn't ready to welcome Katherine with open arms. Not yet.

She drew away from her mother's arms and nodded at Katherine. "I guess so."

Tentatively, Katherine put an arm around Andi's shoulder and led her down the hall and into the library. She closed the doors and sat down on the wide settee. "Would you sit beside me?"

Andi joined her sister, but sat stiffly, prepared for the worst.

"I want to thank you for putting up with us these past few weeks," Katherine said. "I know you resent my being here."

Andi winced as she heard her sister speak the truth. She opened her mouth to speak, but Katherine shook her head and kept talking.

"Mother spends a lot of time with me and the children, and I know it bothers you. And I've seen the hurt in your eyes when the boys and I are laughing over old times—times you can't share. Melinda remembers me and enjoys having a big sister around again. But you already have a big sister, and I'm nothing more than a stranger who has turned your family head over heels. I'm sorry, Andi. I truly didn't mean to cause you so much heartache with my return. I would leave if—"

Andi leaped to her feet. "You mustn't leave! It would break Mother's heart. She'd cry, and I couldn't stand that. Besides, Justin would skin me alive if you left on my account. Please don't go."

Katherine smiled and gently returned Andi to her side. She shook her head. "I'm not leaving yet. I just wanted you to know how grateful I am for your patience."

Andi flushed, suddenly ashamed. She hadn't been patient because she wanted to be, only because Justin had insisted and she'd promised Mother she'd try.

"I know my children aren't the best behaved kids in the valley," Katherine was saying. "Levi, especially, has a chip on his shoulder that's begging to be knocked off. I worried that you and he might come to blows those first few days after we arrived."

Andi gave Katherine a tiny smile. "It crossed my mind a couple of times, but Levi's strong for his size, and quick. He would've licked me—just like he did Jacob."

Katherine nodded. "Yes. He's had his share of brawls, I'm sorry to say. Yet you stood up for him this afternoon. I can't imagine why. And you've allowed Betsy to tag along behind you most days. I'd like to thank you for that. It's real nice of you. She talks about you constantly. 'Andi showed me the kittens in the hayloft.' 'Andi let me brush Taffy.' 'When Andi gets home from school, we'll go riding.'" Katherine chuckled. "You get the idea. Betsy needs someone like you to pay attention to her—someone she can look up to. Perhaps you haven't done it joyfully, but she hasn't noticed."

Andi squirmed as the truth stung her conscience. Katherine was right. Most of the time she *hadn't* done it joyfully. She'd been kind to Betsy and Hannah partly because of Justin's scolding and partly because she didn't want to worry her mother. *Please, God,* she prayed silently, *forgive me for my bad attitude. I'm sorry. Help me love my sister and her children. They've had a hard life, and I've been too selfish to care.*

When Andi raised her head, she smiled at Katherine. A real smile. She squeezed her sister's hand. "When you first came, I was so angry. Angry that nobody told me about you, angry that people were gossiping about our family. I didn't want anyone saying I looked like you, because I was ashamed that you're my sister." She shrugged. "But now I . . . well . . . I guess I don't mind so much that you're here. I'm getting used to you. In fact," she admitted slowly, "if you stay much longer, I might even learn to love you."

Katherine reached out and pulled Andi into her arms. For once, Andi didn't try to get away. She let her sister hug her. "You don't know how much that means to me," Katherine whispered, brushing away tears. "I feel much better about leaving the children here while I'm gone."

"What do you mean? You're not leaving."

"I'm going to San Francisco for a couple of weeks."

"Why?"

"Aunt Rebecca has invited us to stay with her for as long as we like."

"I thought you were staying here. Justin told me you could stay as long as you wanted."

"Only until I get settled in the city," Katherine said.

"You can't leave. Mother will cry."

"Mother knows about my plans," Katherine said. "She knows I'm not suited for ranch life. I never have been. It's enough to know that I'm welcome for a visit now and again. I'd like to make arrangements for some kind of employment in the city, before I take the children."

"Are you going by yourself?"

"I'd planned to, but if you don't mind, I'd like to invite Mother along."

Andi frowned, puzzled. "Why would I mind?"

"Because I don't want to hurt you again by taking Mother away from you for two weeks." Suddenly she grasped Andi's hands and grinned. "I just thought of a splendid idea. Why don't you come along? It could be the three of us."

"To visit Aunt Rebecca?" Andi shook her head. "No thanks! I'd rather stay on the ranch and help out with the kids." She stood up and gave her sister's hand a tug. "Come on, Kate. Let's find Mother. I want to see the look on her face when you invite her to go to San Francisco."

Chapter Eleven

AN EMPTY HOUSE

The house felt huge and empty with her mother gone.
"Of course, it really isn't empty," Andi kept telling herself.
"Far from it." Luisa and Nila still bustled about, performing their
usual tasks. Andi's brothers were in and out. Katherine's children had
made themselves at home, and the clamor of their crashing feet and
high-pitched squeals kept everything in an uproar. Yet to Andi, the
house was empty without her mother's strong, calming influence and
matter-of-fact management. Andi missed her a lot.

With Mother gone, Melinda slid effortlessly into the position of
mistress of the house. With obvious delight, she oversaw the running
of the household, planned the meals, and tried to keep Betsy and
Hannah corralled—not an easy task. More than once, Andi came
home from school to find her sister locked in a battle of wills with
Betsy. It was clear which aunt the little girl preferred. Her tears and
temper tantrums ceased the moment Andi arrived home. Unfortu-
nately, this meant Andi found herself with a tagalong for the rest of
the afternoon and evening.

During this time, the weather changed for the worse, turning
summer's dust into ankle-deep mud when it rained, which it did for a
solid week. The streets of Fresno were dotted with puddles and thick
with the sloppy mire.

"Will the term never end?" Andi picked her way with Levi across
muddy Tulare Street to Justin's office for a ride home after school.
They'd already been forced to cross four other streets, and their shoes

were caked with mud. She glanced up. The wind was blowing; dark clouds scudded across the sky. It looked as if it might rain any minute. Andi shivered and pulled her cloak tighter around herself.

"Just a few more days," Levi said cheerfully. He leaped onto the boardwalk in front of Justin's office and grinned. "I like this weather. It makes mighty good mud balls." He reached down and scooped up a glob of the sticky stuff from the street with his bare hands. "Watch."

Fascinated, Andi watched Levi form a small ball. His hands oozed with mud. Dirty water seeped between his fingers and dripped onto his britches. "What're you going to do with it?" she asked, leaning against a post. "Tim won't let you in Justin's office all muddy like that."

Levi shrugged. "You watch." He patted his mud ball and carefully held it behind his back. Then he leaned against a lamppost near Andi and waited.

Andi gave him a puzzled look and opened her mouth to speak, but Levi put a finger to his lips. Several minutes later, he straightened up, took aim, and hurled the ball of mud across the street.

Splat! The mud landed against the neck of a nicely dressed gentleman just leaving the land office. With a startled cry, the man peered behind his shoulder, slapped wildly at the mud plastered on his neck, and whirled around.

"Levi!" Andi whispered in a choked voice. He'd hit Matthew Powers, Jacob's father. She tore her astonished gaze from the mud dripping down the man's back and looked for Levi. He'd disappeared.

Andi backed against the door to Justin's office and watched Mr. Powers turn a wary look up and down Tulare Street. His face was bright red; he looked ready to burst. *What if he crosses the street and asks me if I saw who did it?* Fearing he might, she fumbled for the doorknob and gave it a hasty turn. Then she hurried into the office and slammed the door shut. Without a word to Justin's clerk, she crossed the room, sat down in a chair, and stared at the floor.

"Well?" Tim demanded from his desk.

"I'm waiting for Justin. It's—it's cold outside."

Tim grunted and returned to his work.

A few minutes later, the door opened and in walked Levi. His hands and face were clean, and most of the mud had been scraped from his britches. Only a few dark streaks remained. His eyes sparkled merrily. He took a seat beside Andi, folded his hands in his lap, and looked at her.

Andi glanced at Tim, who appeared to be ignoring them. Then she leaned toward Levi and whispered in his ear, "Are you *loco?* Matthew Powers, of all people."

"Serves him right for sticking his nose in and making my mother cry." He gave Andi a warm, friendly grin—the first real smile she'd ever received from him. "I did it for you, too. That ol' fool wanted to see you thrashed, sure as shootin'."

Andi didn't know how to respond to Levi's words. On the one hand, he'd plastered an innocent bystander with a mud ball and should be scolded. On the other hand, he'd just offered her the one thing she never thought she'd receive from him: friendship.

She chose the latter.

"Looks like another storm's coming up," Chad announced that evening. He tossed his hat aside and strode into the library, where the rest of the family had gathered to read the paper or play games. With a teasing scowl, he bent over the checkerboard and solemnly pronounced judgment on the game. "Little sister, you are in a heap of trouble. One wrong move and Levi will jump a good number of your pieces."

Andi lifted a red checker.

Chad cringed. "Not that one."

"Uncle Chad! No fair!" Levi protested. "You can't help her."

"Don't worry, Levi," Andi said. "I never pay Chad any mind when it comes to checkers. I beat him 'most every time." She smiled smugly at her brother, who shrugged and sank into a large, overstuffed chair by the fire. He picked up the *Expositor* and began reading, a sure sign he had no idea how the checkers game would end.

"Finish your move," Levi said sourly.

Andi plunked her checker down and sat back to wait. Just as she'd hoped, Levi stumbled into her trap. He jumped her piece with a quiet laugh. Like lightning, Andi moved in for the kill. She jumped the boy's remaining pieces, collected them, and tossed them into the box. "I win."

Levi folded his arms across his chest and sulked. "You always win."

"Not always. Just most of the time. Another game?"

"Not me." He stood up and wandered over to watch as Mitch painstakingly cleaned a rifle.

Andi gathered up the rest of the checkers, relieved at Levi's mellow reaction to losing the game. The first time he'd lost—less than a month ago—he'd overturned the board into Andi's lap, shoved her to the floor, and stormed away, swearing. Over the past few weeks, however, a subtle change had come over him. He no longer cussed, and his bad moods came further and further apart. Since the day Andi had offered to take his whipping, he hadn't once called her "auntie." She was actually beginning to enjoy spending time with her nephew.

She glanced over to see Levi's brown head bent close to Mitch's blond one. They appeared to be in a deep discussion about rifles. Levi pointed to something and laughed. Mitch reached out and tousled the boy's hair.

Poor Levi, Andi realized suddenly. *He hasn't got a father. He hasn't any big brothers, either. No wonder Mitch spends so much time with him.*

"Andi." Justin's voice pulled her from her musing. "The clock struck nine. You and the younger ones better be getting to bed."

Andi pulled herself from her comfortable spot near the checker-board and stood up. At the same time, Melinda gathered up a sleeping Hannah and started for the stairs.

"Want me to take Betsy?" Andi offered.

Melinda nodded gratefully.

"I'll see Levi to bed in a minute," Mitch called from across the room.

A sleepy Betsy slid from the settee and took Andi's hand. Before long, the little girl was settled in the room she shared with Hannah. Andi stumbled wearily into her own bed and curled up under the bed coverings.

Some time later, a deep, low rumble woke Andi from a sound sleep. She didn't know how late it was, but her room was pitch black. Suddenly, a pale light flashed through the French doors leading to the balcony. Another distant rumble followed.

Andi pulled the covers over her head. A thunderstorm! She knew it was far away, up in the hills, but that knowledge couldn't chase away her fear. When she was little, she had often rushed to her parents' room and thrown herself into their bed during a thunderstorm. Well, her mother wasn't here now, and she doubted anyone else would appreciate a midnight visitor. She clapped her hands over her ears as the rumble of thunder came closer.

Another loud crash yanked Andi from beneath her covers. She sat up and peered through the gloom. Her bedroom door hung open. A flash of lightning revealed Betsy trembling and crying in the doorway.

Andi held out her arms. A clap of thunder propelled Betsy into action. She flew across the room and sailed into Andi's bed. Together, the two girls buried themselves under the covers and waited for the storm to pass.

"I'm scared," Betsy whimpered as another roll of thunder sounded.

"It's a long ways off," Andi assured both Betsy and herself. "It won't come here."

"What if it does?" Betsy asked in a quivering voice. "Back home, the thunder made me scream. It shook the whole house. Once, lightning came down the chimney." She started crying in earnest.

Andi wanted to cry too. She hated thunderstorms. But she had to be brave for Betsy's sake. "Well, then," she said, keeping her voice calm and reassuring, "let's pretend we're hiding in a deep cave under the mountains. The thunder and lightning can't get us there. We'll be two little black bears hibernating for the winter. We'll cuddle up together and fall asleep in our warm cave, where the storm can't come. When we wake up, it'll be spring."

Betsy stopped crying. Clearly, the game of being a little black bear cub interested her. "What're our names?" she wanted to know. Her voice no longer trembled.

Slowly, Andi wove an exciting tale of two mischievous bear cubs named Cuffy and Jasper. By the time the rumbling faded and the storm moved deeper into the mountains, Betsy was sound asleep, no doubt dreaming of baby bears and warm caves.

Andi folded back the quilt and breathed in the fresh air. Against the French doors of her balcony, she heard the welcome pattering of raindrops. With a weary sigh, she curled up next to Betsy, pulled the covers around her shoulders, and fell asleep to the music of rain against glass.

Chapter Twelve

A VISIT FROM T. J.

When's Mother coming home?" Andi asked at breakfast the
next morning. She speared a slab of ham and slid it onto her
plate. "It's been weeks."

"Honestly, Andi," Melinda said, "she's only been gone eight days.
I expect they'll be home in another week."

"Another week?" Andi sighed. "It shouldn't take that long to
find a position and visit Aunt Rebecca. Mother's got to be home for
Thanksgiving, and that's next Thursday." She studied her slice of
ham. "You and Nila cook ham fine, but only Mother knows how to
do the turkey right."

"She'll be here in time," Melinda assured her. "Don't you like the
way I'm running the house?"

"Oh, sure." Andi waved the question away. "You're doing a terrific
job. I just miss Mother at night. Especially last night."

Justin chuckled and took a sip of coffee. "That doesn't surprise me,
knowing your fondness for thunderstorms."

"Me an' Andi *hate* thunderstorms," Betsy piped up. "We slept in
a deep, dark cave, where the thunder couldn't get us."

"I'm glad to hear that, Betsy." Justin smiled at the little girl. He
dropped his napkin onto the table and stood up. "I see Chad and
Mitch have already left. Is Levi with them?"

Andi nodded. "He asked me early this morning to go riding with
him, but it's such a dreary day that I didn't want to go. Mitch said
Levi could follow the hands around and watch them repair fences."

"Sounds exciting," Justin said, in a voice that meant the opposite. "I've got some paperwork to take care of this morning, so I'll be in the library." He smiled at Melinda. "Delicious breakfast, honey. Give my compliments to the cook."

Melinda beamed. "Nila was busy with the churning, so I did the cooking this morning."

"I thought so." He left the dining room, whistling.

An hour later, Andi wished she'd taken Levi up on his offer to go riding. There was absolutely nothing of interest going on in the yard. She and Betsy had brushed and groomed Taffy until she shone. Andi had done all her Saturday chores: fed and watered the stabled horses, collected the eggs with Betsy's help, and taken the newly churned butter to the springhouse, but the morning threatened to drag on for hours.

She was in the corral, showing Betsy how to put a bridle on a small, chocolate-colored pony, when a cheerful voice called out a greeting.

Andi whirled and saw T. J. Silver making his way across the yard. "T. J.! Howdy." She was delighted to see him. "You working for us? Did Sid give you a job? Whatcha been doing?"

T. J. grinned through his shaggy beard. He held up a hand and called out, "Hold on. One question at a time, please."

Andi quickly helped Betsy into the saddle of her pony and handed her the reins. "Here you go. Don't be afraid. Coco can't get out. You can ride him around and around as much as you like."

Betsy slammed her heels into the pony's flank and shouted, but the little animal merely turned his head and looked at her. Then he carefully picked up his hooves and plodded slowly around the inside of the corral fence. Betsy squealed her delight.

T. J. laughed and joined Andi at the corral fence. "That little pony sure don't let much excite him."

"Nope. He's old and set in his ways. No matter how hard Betsy kicks him, he won't break into anything faster than a trot."

"A good first pony," T. J. said.

"He was mine," Andi said. She climbed over the corral fence and jumped to the ground. "And Melinda's, and Mitch's." She grinned. "All of us had Coco for our first pony. Justin named him."

T. J. nodded toward Betsy. "Is she your little sister?"

"No, she's Levi's sister. You remember Levi?"

"The spunky young fella who chased after you up by the creek?" When Andi nodded, T. J. chuckled. "Didn't get a chance to meet him, I'm afraid." He looked around. "Where is he this morning?"

"With Chad and Mitch. I think they're checking fences, or pretending to for Levi's sake. He likes to play cowhand every chance he gets."

T. J. rested his arms across the top rail of the fence and watched Betsy circle the corral. "Cute kid," he remarked. Then he asked, "Your niece and nephew staying with you long?"

Andi boosted herself to the top of the fence. "Only until my sister finds work in San Francisco. That's where she and my mother have been for the past week—looking for work. Kate doesn't like ranches. She wants to live in the city."

T. J. glanced around with approval in his eyes. "This is a fine ranch, Andi. Your sister must be *loco* not to want to stay here."

Andi couldn't have agreed more. Who *wouldn't* want to live in wide, open spaces with sun, fresh air, sweet hay, and horses? It warmed her heart to hear that T. J. felt the same way. "Do you like working for my brothers?" she asked.

"Haven't seen 'em much," T. J. confessed. "But Sid's a good foreman. The work's hard, the pay's good, and the Circle C has the best grub this side of the Sierras." He grinned. "A fella can't ask for more than that."

"What about family?" Andi asked. "You got any?" She knew she was breaking an unspoken rule by asking a hired hand about his past, but she couldn't help it. She'd rescued him from certain death and felt she had the right to know a little bit about him.

It was clear T. J. didn't agree. His eyes narrowed at the question, and he lost his smile. "I had a family . . . once." He turned a dark look on Andi. "Don't ask me about them again."

Andi's mouth fell open. She was about to offer an apology for prying, when Levi's shrill voice split the air.

"Andi! We got a letter from Mama!" He raced his pinto up to Andi and yanked the pony to a stop, waving the letter above his head. Ignoring T. J., he slid from Patches and presented the cream-colored envelope to Andi. "Mitch took me to town to fetch the mail. We opened it, and Mama and Grandmother are coming home day after tomorrow." His huge grin and sparkling eyes told Andi how much he missed his mother.

"Yippee!" Andi shouted her joy. She missed *her* mother too.

"It also says Aunt Rebecca won't hear of Mama taking some low, common job," Levi prattled on. "She wants us to live with her and keep her company. She's gonna send me and Betsy to school and buy all of us new clothes and teach us to be fine, fancy folks." He wrinkled his brow. "Is she rich, Andi?"

"Very rich." Andi glanced at the envelope in her hand. "The letter said all that?"

"Yep. And there's lots more, but Mama said she'd explain when she gets back." He grinned. "I can't wait!"

"I thought you liked living on the ranch," Andi said quietly. Now that it looked like Katherine and the kids were leaving, Andi wasn't sure she wanted them to go.

Levi's face fell. "I do like it here, but I miss the adventure of the city. There's always something exciting happening there." Then he brightened. "Just 'cause I leave don't mean I can't come back for a visit." He snatched up the envelope. "Mama says we're leaving the day after Thanksgiving. I guess that means no more riding or racing. I'm sorta sorry about that."

Andi jumped down from the fence and put an arm around her nephew's shoulder. "Tell you what, Levi. Maybe we can talk Justin into letting us go riding tomorrow after church, if the weather isn't too bad."

Levi nodded. "I gotta beat you at least once before I go." He ducked under Andi's arm, grabbed the reins of his pony, and headed for the barn. "I'm going up to the house to tell Justin and Melinda that Mama's coming home. See ya later."

"Sure," Andi replied. With Levi gone, she turned her attention back to Betsy. The little girl was riding around the corral, completely oblivious to the conversation, kicking Coco and humming a little tune. Andi waved to her and turned to speak to T. J.

He was gone.

Chapter Thirteen

AN AFTERNOON RIDE

U ncle Justin, can me and Andi go riding after dinner?" Levi asked on the way home from church the next day. "I'm not used to sitting still so long—not even in school. It feels like a million spiders are crawling around inside my belly."

"You want to come up and drive the team?" Justin asked.

"Sure!" Levi scrambled over the back of the seat and took his place between Justin and Melinda. "But I still want to go riding," he said as he took the reins.

"Reverend Harris did seem to go on and on today," Melinda agreed with a sigh. "I'm worn out from trying to keep Hannah still."

From the back seat, Andi joined the plea. "Please, Justin? It might be the last chance Levi has to ride around the ranch."

"Please, Uncle Justin?" Betsy added.

Justin chuckled. "All right. You may go—so long as the weather holds."

A chorus of cheers greeted Justin's permission, and the rest of the ride home passed quickly. They pulled into the yard, and Justin brought the matched pair of bay horses to a stop. He climbed down and came around to the other side of the carriage, where he reached up and took Hannah from Melinda. To the child's shrieks of delight, he swung her high in the air then set her gently on her feet.

"Me too!" Betsy demanded, climbing over Andi to get to her uncle.

Justin complied with a grin. When Betsy was safely on the ground, he helped his sisters from the carriage. Levi leaped out of the rig and took off running toward the house. "Come on," he shouted. "I'm hungry."

After a dinner of fried chicken, mashed potatoes and gravy, biscuits, and apple cobbler, Andi felt too full to ride. She stepped out of the house and glanced toward the mountains. A stiff breeze was blowing, driving thick gray clouds up against the foothills.

She shivered. Maybe she didn't want to ride today, after all. "It looks like it's going to rain soon. There's nothing worse than riding in the rain. Let's play checkers instead."

Levi would have none of it. He pointed to a break in the clouds. A sliver of sunlight touched the hills. "It's sunny where we're going, Andi. Please? Justin said we could." He grabbed Andi's hand and looked at her with pleading eyes. "Just a little ride?"

"Oh, all right," Andi gave in. Then she grinned. "You're getting mighty good at sweet-talking, little nephew. All those city girls'll be falling at your feet in no time."

"Don't talk like a sissy girl!" Levi snapped. He thrust Andi's hand aside and stomped off toward the barn, his high spirits clearly dampened.

Andi kicked herself mentally. Levi was actually speaking nicely, and she'd teased him. She ran up behind him and laid an apologetic hand on his shoulder. "I'm sorry. I was just joking. Don't be sore."

Levi turned around and eyed Andi carefully. Then he jerked his chin toward the barn. "Let's ride."

When Betsy and Hannah discovered the two older children were riding without them, they put up such a fuss that Andi was forced to give in. "If it starts raining even one drop, I'll bring everybody home," she promised Justin, who looked ready to change his mind about the afternoon ride.

"All right," he said. "It does look like it's breaking up. But don't be gone long."

"Just up to my spot, throw some rocks in the creek, and back again. A couple of hours?"

Justin nodded. "Two hours."

Andi and Levi saddled their horses and led them out of the barn. By now, the sun had cleared a good portion of clouds from the sky. It shone down warm and friendly, and Levi tossed his heavy jacket aside.

"You'll be sorry," Andi warned, settling herself on Taffy.

Levi ignored her and mounted Patches.

Justin lifted Betsy into Coco's saddle and handed Levi the lead rope. Then he plopped Hannah down in Andi's lap and said, "I want you to remember that these children are your responsibility. You're in charge."

"Sure, Justin." She threw a delighted grin in Levi's direction. He stuck out his tongue at her.

Justin frowned. "I'm serious, Andi. Levi may act like he can take care of himself, but you know the ranch. Use your head to keep everybody out of trouble, all right?"

"Does that mean I have to mind her?" Levi grumbled from his pony's back.

Justin gave Levi a firm look. "That's exactly what it means, young man. Do you think you can do that?"

"I reckon." He shrugged and looked at Andi. "If it's the only way I get to ride today."

"It is," Justin replied with a pleased nod. "Now go on and have a good time. I'll see you later."

Andi nudged Taffy, and the mare took off at a gentle trot.

Hannah squealed her excitement. She raised her hand and waved at Justin. "Bye!" she shouted. "Bye!"

They started out slowly, mostly to give Betsy and her little pony a chance to keep up. Levi brought Patches alongside Taffy and maintained a firm grip on Coco's lead line. Betsy, although she was learning to ride, was still uneasy about riding outside the large corral. Besides, leading Coco was the only way to make the pony go faster than a walk. Betsy held tightly to the saddle horn and didn't complain about being led.

Hannah looked perfectly content. Under one arm, she clutched her doll, Tessie. She sucked her thumb and leaned back into the warmth of Andi's body. Whenever she saw Betsy and Levi draw near, she pulled out her thumb and yelled, "See me! I'm riding. I'm riding."

When they came to a flat place, Andi took the lead rope from Levi and allowed him to run Patches at a full gallop. She watched with admiration. Levi could really ride. He stood up in his stirrups and shouted his usual Indian war whoop, then circled around and pretended to knock Andi off her horse. The little girls screamed their laughter, and Levi began his circle all over again.

They took turns holding Hannah and the lead rope, so Andi could enjoy the opportunity to gallop Taffy through the dry, golden grass.

Andi reined in beside Levi. "What about our race? There's a long, level stretch right near the creek that makes a terrific racetrack. We could leave Betsy and Hannah under a tree for a few minutes. Want to?"

Levi's huge grin was his answer. He jabbed Patches in the sides and took off up a hill. Andi followed, pulling gently on Coco's lead line. She let Hannah hold Taffy's reins until they reached the top of the rise. Taffy knew exactly where to go.

Straight ahead, Andi's favorite spot on the entire ranch opened up. The Sierra Nevada range rose in the distance. Clouds were gathering again, covering the peaks like a thick, fluffy quilt. To the right, the creek gurgled noisily. The recent rains had swelled it nearly to its banks. Oak trees dotted the hills.

Andi sighed. Even in November, this place was beautiful. She reined Taffy to a stop under an old oak tree and slid from the saddle. Then she tied her horse loosely to a branch and lifted Hannah to the ground. The little girl immediately started running alongside the creek.

"Stay away from the creek," Andi warned. "It's cold and deep right now."

Hannah obediently skipped back a few steps. Betsy joined her. They picked up rocks and began tossing them into the water as if it were the grandest game in the world. Levi joined Andi and grinned at her. "So, are we going to race or what?"

Andi nodded eagerly and called to the girls. "Come over here and sit down a minute. Levi and I are going to race. You get to decide who wins."

The girls hurried over and plopped themselves under the tree. "I'll say *go*," Betsy said. She reached out and grasped her little sister's hand. "And I'll make sure Hannah doesn't run off and get drowned."

"Good girl," Andi praised her. "We'll only be a few minutes." She untied Taffy's reins from the branch and mounted. Then she pointed to a huge, ancient oak a couple hundred yards away. "We race to the tree, go around it, then back to this spot. That way Betsy can see who passes the finish line first. Fair?"

Levi nodded. "Fair enough." He hunkered down in the saddle and gripped the reins.

Andi did the same. "Ready, Betsy?"

Betsy nodded. "Ready—*go!*" she shouted.

The two horses took off. Andi was more experienced at racing and had the better horse. However, Levi was lighter, and Patches looked determined to give the mare a run for her money. They reached the oak; Andi rounded it slightly ahead of Levi. Levi caught up as they galloped the last fifty yards, and they raced neck-and-neck past the tree where they'd left the little girls.

Levi shrieked his delight. "Did I win?"

"It was close." Andi met Levi as he reined Patches to a stop. "I think it was a tie. Want to race again?"

"You bet," Levi agreed wholeheartedly. "I'm sure Patches will win by a length this time, now that he knows the lay of the land."

Andi laughed. "Let's check with the girls first. Betsy's supposed to be judging this race."

She turned Taffy around and loped back to the tree. "Betsy," she called out merrily. "Who won the—?"

She broke off and yanked Taffy to a stop. Clutching the reins, she stared at the empty spot under the tree.

Betsy and Hannah were gone.

Chapter Fourteen

A DANGEROUS DISCOVERY

L evi pulled up beside Andi and stammered, "Th-they're gone."
"I can see that!" Andi snapped at Levi and tried to breathe. It felt as if a giant fist were squeezing the air from her lungs. Her heart raced. Gasping, she tumbled from Taffy's back and hit the ground with a *thud*. Then she raced to the creek. "Betsy! Hannah!" she screamed. There was no answer.

Oh, God, where are they? She stood on the bank, her gaze riveted on the roiling, swirling water. A sob caught in her throat. She shouldn't have left the girls alone, not even for a minute. Justin had trusted her to look after them. *Please don't let them be in the creek!* she prayed silently.

Levi ran up and grabbed Andi's arm. "What're we going to do, Andi? We can't just stand here. We gotta find 'em. What if they fell in the—?"

"Shut up and let me think!" Fear made her words harsh. She shook Levi off and tried to come up with a plan. But she couldn't think. She could only stare numbly at the muddy water sloshing over her boot tops. Her stomach felt tied in knots.

"They're right here, safe and sound," a voice called over the noise of the creek.

Andi spun around. Tears sprang to her eyes at the sight of a tall, handsome man leading Betsy and Hannah toward her.

"I didn't want these two little ones to fall in the creek," the man said with a friendly grin, "so I took 'em for a walk."

Andi rushed over and gathered the girls in a tearful embrace. Hannah was crying, and Betsy looked close to tears. "Don't cry. You're all right." She buried her face in their silky hair and hugged them tight. Then she took a deep breath and glanced up at the man standing over her. "You scared me half to death, mister. Didn't you see Levi and me racing? We were in plain sight." She straightened up and faced him. "I mean . . . well . . . it's not that I'm not grateful, but I think the girls were perfectly safe where we left them. You needn't . . ." Her voice trailed off, and she looked at the man in confusion. He seemed strangely familiar. "Who are you, anyway?"

"It's me, Andi," the man replied with a chuckle. "T. J." He spread his arms and turned a full circle. "I used my first week's pay yesterday afternoon to buy some new clothes, get a shave, and clean up. What do you think?"

Andi wasn't ready to forgive T. J. for scaring her so badly. "I think it was downright mean of you to take the girls for a walk. Why didn't you wait with them under the tree?"

Before T. J. could answer, Levi came alongside Andi and gave her hand a tug. "Let's go," he whispered. "Right now."

"We just got here." Andi peeled his fingers from her hand. "The girls are safe. T. J. was with them. He's the fella I told you about. The one we found up here a few weeks back. He's working for us now."

Levi shook his head. "I want to go home. Now."

T. J. crossed his arms over his chest and looked at Levi. "What's the matter with you, boy? There's no call to go running off. Haven't seen you for quite a spell. How are you?" When Levi didn't answer, T. J. lowered his arms to his sides and took a step forward. "Answer me."

"I'm f-fine, Pa," Levi stuttered, stepping back. He yanked on Andi's sleeve. "Please, Andi. Let's go home."

Andi didn't move. She couldn't. She stood frozen, staring at T. J. and trying to make sense of what Levi had just said. *Pa? That can't be right.* "What's going on?" she said. "Why did Levi call you his pa?"

"Because that's who I am."

Andi's heart plunged clear to her toes. "You . . . you said your name was T. J. Silver."

He shrugged. "T. J., Troy. What's the difference?" Then he grinned. "The look on your face is precious, Andi. Don't you realize a name is the easiest thing in the world to change?" He ran a hand through his hair. "The rest was a bit more difficult—the hair, my beard. But that run-in with those ruffians worked to my advantage, although I could have done without the knifing." His smile grew wider at Andi's astonishment.

"Why?" She drew the two little girls close. "Why didn't you tell me your real name?"

"And give myself away?" T. J. shook his head. "Not a chance. The minute I opened my eyes and saw you, I knew I was on the Circle C. You look enough like my Katie to be her twin sister. Even if she wasn't on the ranch, I knew she'd show up eventually. I wanted to lay low 'til I was ready."

"Ready for what?" Andi already knew the answer.

"Don't pretend you don't know. I've come for my family. Thanks to your willingness to bring me supplies and keep my presence a secret, I was able to rest and regain my strength. Then when I saw Levi at the creek, I knew Katie was here. I disguised myself the best I could and tried to stay clear of the kids. I used the job you helped me find as an excuse to stick around the ranch, so I could discover the best way to get my wife and kids back."

He walked over and clapped a hand on Levi's shoulder. "I've got plans for us, boy. Big plans. In a few days your mother will meet us, and we can be a family again."

"What if she doesn't want to?" Andi gathered Hannah into her arms and lifted her up. Betsy hung onto Andi's riding skirt and stared at T. J.

T. J.'s look turned dark. "She doesn't have a choice. I don't take kindly to my wife running off with my kids. It's taken me a long time to track her down. When I figured out she'd crawled back to her family, I had a good laugh. She must have been desperate if she humbled herself enough to beg your forgiveness." He drew his lips into a sneer. "Wish I could have seen her—the once-proud Katherine Carter—pleading for a place to stay."

Andi erupted into fury. "We should have left you in the creek!"

T. J. laughed. "True enough, but I know you wouldn't have done it. You have a kind heart, and you're entirely too trusting. Your friends had the right of it the day you found me. You should have listened to them and been a little more suspicious." He shrugged. "Anyway, I want to thank you for delivering my children to me." He gave her a mocking bow.

Andi felt dizzy with horror. *What have I done?* She looked at Levi. "I'm sorry, Levi. I didn't know."

"It's not your fault," Levi said bitterly. "You got fooled. My pa's real good at it; he makes his living swindling folks. You didn't have a chance." He let out a long, disgusted breath. "I wish I'd paid attention that day at the creek. I would've recognized him—beard or no beard—if you'd given me half a chance. But you were in such an all-fired hurry to send me back to the ranch. Now it's—"

"Enough chatter. Let's go." T. J. glared at Levi and yanked Betsy to his side. She burst into tears. "Once Katie knows I have the kids, she'll come running. She won't leave them with me, and that's a fact."

"T. J.," Andi pleaded, "please. Let's go back to the ranch. When Kate gets home from—"

"My name's Troy," he corrected her, "and I'm not going back to the ranch. Your brothers would probably shoot me on sight." He kept a firm grip on Betsy, who was sobbing in earnest. "Stop that sniveling, Elizabeth. I can't hear to think."

"I want Andi," Betsy wailed. She twisted around and planted a sharp kick on her father's shin.

Troy tossed Betsy aside with a curse. She scrambled to Andi and threw her arms around her waist. "I wanna go home. I want Mama."

Troy motioned to Levi and pointed toward the creek. "My horse is tied up in that clump of scrub oak near the creek. Go get him."

Levi sprang away. A few minutes later, he returned, leading Troy's horse. Without a word, he brought the gelding to a halt in front of his father and waited, shivering with cold. His hands and clothes were black with mud.

Troy snatched the reins from the boy's hands. "What happened?"

Levi cringed. "I t-tripped and f-fell," he explained through chattering teeth.

"Can't you do anything right?" Troy wrenched Hannah from Andi's arms, mounted his horse, and plopped the little girl down in front of him. Hannah howled.

"What have you Carters done to my kids?" Troy bellowed. "They're nothing but a passel of sniveling, wailing brats. Even Levi looks scared."

Levi flinched at the tone in his father's voice but held his ground. He wrapped his arms around himself for warmth.

"Maybe they're scared of *you*," Andi shot back. She was shaking with fury and helplessness. This was all her fault. She'd been tricked by this man's warm and friendly manner, just as he'd most likely intended right from the start. She wanted to scream at somebody, and Troy was handy. "You're nothing but a dirty, rotten swindler, and I'm glad my sister finally figured it out. Hanging's too good for a low-down skunk like you."

Troy brought his horse alongside Andi and leaned over. With a quick, sharp *smack*, the palm of his hand connected with Andi's face. "Watch your mouth, little sister."

Andi reeled backward, stunned. How dare he hit her! She clenched her fists. "I'm *not* your little sister, and don't you ever touch me again."

Blinking back angry tears, she stomped over to Levi, who was gaping at her with awe and respect. "I told you that you'd be sorry if you left your jacket at home," she scolded him. She pulled off her own warm jacket and helped stuff Levi's soggy arms through the sleeves.

"A real good little Samaritan, aren't you?" Troy sneered and turned to Levi. "Mount up, son."

Levi stared at his father. "B-but I'm c-cold."

"The sooner we get going, the sooner we'll get to someplace warm and dry. Now, do as I say or you'll feel the back of my hand."

Levi shuffled over to Patches and pulled himself into the saddle. He gathered up the reins and brought the horse alongside Troy.

"Andi," Troy said, "put Betsy on the pony and bring me the lead rope."

"And if I don't?"

"Well, I've got no reason to be nice to you any longer. If I get off this horse, you'll get more than a slap on the cheek for your sass."

"Do like he says, Andi." Levi sounded defeated. "As long as my pa's in a good mood, everything's fine. Don't put him in a bad mood, or else . . ." His voice trailed off when Troy shot him a mean look.

Andi glanced at Betsy, who was trembling with uncertainty. She looked up at Hannah sitting in Troy's lap. With her thumb in her mouth, the little girl was whimpering and watching Andi's every move with her round, blue eyes.

"All right," Andi finally agreed. She led Coco to Troy and handed him the rope. Then she boosted Betsy onto the back of the pony. "Don't be afraid," she whispered in her ear. "God will take care of us. He'll see to it that you don't fall off Coco." She kissed Betsy's cheek and smiled. "Hang on tight and stick close to me. Everything's going to be fine."

"Promise?"

"You bet!" But her smile faded as she walked back to Taffy, and she mounted with a heavy heart. So far, nothing was fine. She had failed utterly in her responsibility. Here she was, stuck with a new, mean Troy and three little kids, and no idea where they were headed. She gathered up the reins and brought Taffy alongside Betsy. "We're ready," she told Troy.

"You're not coming," he said.

"Yes, I am. I promised Justin I'd—"

"No." Troy cut her off. "You're going home to deliver a message. If I overheard you and Levi right, Kate will be back tomorrow. You tell her to meet me in Denver, one week from today. She knows where. I'll have the kids with me."

"Justin put me in charge of the kids. I can't leave them."

"You do what I say, or I'll take your horse and leave you here."

"Then you'll hang as a horse thief, for sure." She glared at her brother-in-law, daring him to make her leave.

For an instant, Troy looked like he wanted to shake her. Then he cracked a smile, which quickly gave way to a low chuckle. "You Carters sure got more than your fair share of stubbornness, but it's not going to help you today." He glanced at the sky. "It's starting to cloud up again. Looks like a storm's moving in." He paused and lost his smile. "What's it going to be—a long, miserable walk home or a chance to ride? I don't care which you choose."

Andi knew she was outmatched. Troy was bigger than she was. If he took Taffy, she'd be stranded. At all costs, she must keep her horse. She tightened her grip on the reins and glared at Troy. He grinned, clearly pleased at having bested her.

"Good-bye, Levi," Andi said. She blinked furiously. "Take care of Betsy and Hannah."

Levi wiped his eyes and nose and said nothing.

Betsy started crying.

"Nandi!" Hannah wailed. "No go!" She raised her arms toward Andi, but Troy shoved them down. "Nandi! Mama!" Her shrieks filled the air.

Andi turned Taffy around and came alongside Troy. "I'm sorry, Hannah. I can't go with you right now. But . . ." She carefully drew her locket from around her neck and held it out. "Here. This is for you and Tessie."

Hannah's cries ceased instantly. She reached out a tentative hand and curled her small fingers around the heart-shaped locket. "Lecklace," she said softly. "*My* lecklace." She looked at Andi hopefully.

Andi nodded and let go of the chain. It fell into Hannah's lap. "Yes, Hannah. The necklace is yours, but only if you promise to stop crying and be a good girl until you see your mama again."

Hannah looked up at Andi and smiled through her tears.

Andi's heart squeezed with love for the little girl. Hannah was no longer the irritating pest Andi had once considered her, but an adorable child with golden curls and a dimple in each cheek. Her blue eyes showed her love for her aunt. With all her heart, Andi wished Hannah could once more destroy her room or throw a temper tantrum—anything to keep her on the ranch and out of Troy's reach.

"My lecklace," Hannah said firmly. "Tessie's lecklace." She pulled her doll from under her arm and gently placed the chain around her neck. Then she leaned against her father's chest, popped her thumb in her mouth, and was silent.

Troy looked from Hannah to Andi and let out a sigh of relief. "That's better."

"I did it for Hannah," Andi said, "not for you."

"Well, whatever your reason, at least you shut her up." He tipped his hat in farewell, gave Coco's lead line a jerk, and headed out.

Andi sat helplessly on Taffy and watched Troy and the children disappear into the oak trees covering the hillside. A stiff breeze whipped across her face, and she shivered. She already missed her warm jacket. If she didn't start for home soon, she was going to get mighty cold and wet.

She shook herself free of such thoughts. "I can't go home. You hear me, Taffy? I can't. I could never face Kate . . . or Justin. I've got to go after the kids and bring them home. Are you going to help me?"

Taffy tossed her head and snorted, clearly ready to do anything but stand around in an empty field the rest of the afternoon.

Andi sighed. She wished she hadn't been in such a hurry to give away her jacket. "Well then, girl, I guess we'd better get going."

Chapter Fifteen

THE STORM

Andi knew she'd made the right decision about tracking Troy and the children, but she wasn't happy about it. Troy would be furious when he discovered he was being followed. How would he react? She had other concerns, as well. Even if she did manage to find the kids, how would she get them away from their father?

And then there was this miserable weather!

She glanced at the sky. Storm clouds were rolling in, piling up against the mountains in great heaps. Soon it would rain, washing out any tracks Troy and the kids might have left. "Oh, God," she quickly prayed, "please keep the rain away until I figure out where they've gone."

Andi nudged Taffy into a trot and wound her way through the oaks, where she had last seen the group traveling. Tracks were easy to find. The ground was soft from the recent rains, and three horses' hooves chewed up the old, wet mixture of grass and dirt fairly well.

For the first few miles, it looked as if Troy had circled back to follow the creek. Later on, he'd taken off cross-country, heading northwest. Andi almost missed the turn in the fading light. The trail led off into a gully between two hills, then up again, north for a few miles, then west. Where in the world was Troy taking the children? There was nothing up here but lonely rangeland and a line shack or two.

"Maybe he's going to spend the night in a line shack," Andi reasoned. It wasn't a bad choice. The line shacks were kept stocked and ready for any tired cowhand working far from the home ranch.

Andi hoped this was the case. She was cold and hungry, and it was getting darker by the hour. Great, black clouds raced overhead, threatening rain. A few hard, cold drops fell against her cheeks. She impatiently brushed them aside. Peering down, she could barely make out the tracks in the dim light. She'd be stuck out here in the middle of a chilly November night before long. Not a pleasant prospect.

The sound of running water brought Andi to a halt. She pulled back on Taffy's reins and slid from the saddle. Kneeling beside a small creek, she saw the faint tracks of at least one horse that had crossed. She stood up and sighed. This had to be the creek that ran close to the northern boundaries of the ranch. But what was north of the ranch?

"The river," she said aloud. The San Joaquin River, flowing south and west out of the mountains, was only a few miles away. "Wait a minute." Andi snapped her fingers and quickly mounted Taffy. "That abandoned town is up here, right next to the river. Troy would remember Millerton," she told her horse. Talking to Taffy always helped her think things through. "There's got to be a few empty buildings left." She was certain Troy would find an old cabin—one that had been spared from past flooding—and spend the night. The next day, he'd—

"He'd what?" Andi asked Taffy as she urged the palomino across the creek. "Where would he go next?" She chewed on her lip, trying to solve the puzzle. Denver was a far cry from the foothills of the Sierra Nevada. How would he get back into the valley to catch the train? He certainly wouldn't chance backtracking to Fresno.

The gurgling of the creek gave Andi the answer. "That's it, Taffy! All he has to do is cross the river. From there, it's less than twenty miles to Madera, over easy ground." Her heart beat fast at the revelation. Surely Troy wouldn't try to cross the river with three children. The rain was filling the streams and rivers to their banks.

More than ever, Andi felt the need to find Levi and the girls. But night was falling fast. Could she locate Millerton in the dark? Three or four miles were a long way over rough country. A few more drops splattered against her face. She shivered and lowered her head against the chilly breeze.

She was so cold and tired that she missed the sudden change in Taffy's gait. It took her a minute to realize they were no longer struggling up yet another hill filled with scratchy brush and an occasional oak or lonely pine. Taffy was trotting along at a fair pace on a level track.

Andi looked down. Beneath her lay an old road. It was overgrown with dead grass and brush, but she could see the faint outline of wheel ruts. She looked up. The road led northwest, straight toward the old town site.

"You found it, Taffy!" She now knew exactly where she was. This road had once been part of an old stage line that stretched from Stockton, through Millerton, and down to Visalia, hugging the Sierra foothills for miles. When the townsfolk abandoned Millerton several years ago and moved to Fresno, the stage no longer traveled this section of the state. But Andi and Cory had ridden here many times during their explorations around the ranch.

Andi guessed Troy knew as well as she did the path this road took through the ranch. "In fact, he's probably used it quite a bit these past few weeks," she muttered with a stab of annoyance. "I betcha anything Troy's holed up in a cabin around here, snug as you please, in front of a warm fire."

The thought made Andi shiver. She nudged Taffy into a slow, loping gait and gave the mare her head. Taffy was sure-footed. She wouldn't leave the road if she could help it. Even in the fading light, the mare would bring Andi safely to the river and the abandoned town.

Andi was so pleased to be on the right track that she didn't notice when the small smattering of raindrops changed to a steady downpour.

Then the clouds burst open and rain spilled out in great bucketfuls. Within moments, she was drenched. A gust of wind drove the rain into her face. She clenched her teeth to keep them from chattering. "Come on, girl," she urged Taffy. "Let's find a place to get out of this storm."

Without warning, a flash of lightning lit up the sky, followed instantly by an earsplitting crack of thunder.

Taffy bolted.

Andi lost the reins and nearly flew from the saddle. With a cry of alarm, she clutched the saddle horn, hunkered down, and let Taffy run. She hadn't counted on a thunderstorm right over her head. Rain, yes. But this? Thunder and lightning were scary enough at home, when she could take refuge under her bedcovers, but here there was no place to hide. She swallowed her terror and hung on.

Taffy gradually slowed to a nervous trot. Andi fumbled for the reins. Murmuring words she hoped would quiet her horse and calm her own racing heart, she sat up and brought Taffy to a halt. The mare danced around and tossed her head in protest.

"Easy, girl." Andi swiped at the water running down her face. She wished she'd worn a hat! She peered through the dark, hoping to find a place where she could get out of the rain. But she saw only black clouds, black rain, the black outline of a few scraggly trees, and the black road.

"Oh, T-taffy," she stammered between chattering teeth, "I wish I'd never d-done this. I'm cold. I'm wet. And I'm s-scared. I'll never find them." She choked back a sob. "I won't cry. I *won't!*"

Another bolt of lightning flashed. Thunder crashed. Taffy whinnied and reared up. Andi tumbled from the saddle and landed in the middle of the muddy road. Instantly she leaped to her feet and snatched at the dangling reins. "Stand still, Taffy."

Taffy refused to stand still. She shied away, threw her head back, and tried to break free from Andi's tight grip. It was clear the mare didn't understand why she was being forced to endure such a storm, especially in the dark.

"Whoa, girl." Andi knew she must try to soothe her friend. "I'm right here. I'm sorry I startled you by falling off." Her thoughts were screaming, but she forced her voice to remain calm. Reaching out, she stroked Taffy's neck and kept talking. "I hate thunderstorms, and I see that you do, too. We'll never do *this* again, I promise.

"Another thing. When we get home, you've got to keep quiet about what just happened. I'll never hear the end of it if anybody finds out you dumped me."

Taffy began to settle down at the soothing words. She snorted, tossed her head a few more times, and then stood still. "Good girl." Andi patted her horse's quivering flank. "Take it easy. We'll find shelter in no time. Be patient." She gathered up the reins and reached for the stirrup just as another flash of lightning tore open the sky.

It was too much for Taffy. She was a good horse, Andi's best friend and loyal companion. Yet even the best horse has limits. It became clear in a matter of seconds that Taffy had reached the end of her endurance. She tore the reins from Andi's hands and took off into the night.

"Taffy, come back here!"

It was no use. For the first time in Andi's memory, her beloved horse was running away. Running home. Taffy flew down the road as if a starving mountain lion were after her. Reins flapped wildly across her shoulders. Stirrups bounced against her sides. Still she ran. Taffy clearly had no intention of stopping until she reached her warm, dry stable.

Andi stood shivering in the middle of the old road and started to cry. Her horse was gone. She was all alone and chilled to the bone. The wind drove the freezing rain through her clothing like it was made of tissue paper. What now?

She wiped the rain and tears from her face. "Please, God," she sobbed, "I've got to find shelter soon. I don't think I can make it out here in the storm much longer. I'm so cold and—"

Before she finished her desperate prayer, a flicker of yellow caught her gaze. She rubbed her eyes and squinted toward the pale, twinkling light. Off the road to her left, almost hidden in a cluster of oak and scrub pine, a cabin nestled on a small rise. At least Andi *thought* it was a cabin. When she looked again, the flicker became a small square. A window?

When another flash of lightning lit up the sky, Andi could make out the dark outline of a cabin not more than twenty yards away. Her heart leaped. Ignoring the thunder, she abandoned the road and raced up the incline. She sloshed her way through the rivulets of water pouring past her and quickly found herself less than a dozen feet from her goal.

Caution brought her to a halt. What would Troy say when he saw her? Worse, what if this was the wrong place? It could very well be a hermit's cabin, someone who didn't care for visitors. What if—?

The storm decided for her. Lightning and thunder ripped the air once more, and Andi threw caution to the wind. She dashed up to the door of the crude little cabin, lifted the latch, and burst through the opening.

The warmth of the tiny place engulfed her. She crumpled to the floor in a soggy heap and lay still. Letting out a grateful sigh, she closed her eyes and didn't care what happened to her next, so long as she was out of the rain.

Chapter Sixteen

A CHILLY WELCOME

Clamoring voices and the feel of many hands tugging at her roused Andi from her dazed state. She opened her eyes. Levi knelt beside her on the floor, plucking at her sleeve. When he caught her eye, he shook his head and grinned. "You're stupid," he said cheerfully.

Troy pushed his children aside and yanked Andi to her feet. "Of all the outrageous, reckless stunts!" He swore and gave her a shake. "I told you to go home."

Andi's teeth chattered so hard she couldn't speak. Fresh tears welled up. She didn't bother to wipe them away.

Troy shoved her aside and stomped across the room, muttering under his breath. "Fool kid, tryin' to get herself killed."

Andi collapsed to the floor, shivering with fear and cold. Troy looked angry. Scary angry. Perhaps this hadn't been such a good idea, after all. What if he decided to throw her out of the cabin and lock the door? She couldn't go back out in that storm.

Small arms encircled her neck and hugged her tightly. "I'm glad you're here," Betsy whispered in her ear.

"You've got to get out of those wet clothes," Troy growled, dropping a bundle of clothing beside her. He grabbed her arm and pulled her roughly to her feet. "Betsy, bring the dry clothes."

Betsy reached down and snatched up the bundle. She hurried after her father as he half-dragged, half-carried Andi to the door leading to a small lean-to. With a crash, he kicked it open and thrust her through the opening. "Change as fast as you can and get back to the fire, before you freeze to death." Troy turned on his heel and left the lean-to, slamming the door so hard the little building shook.

Andi gulped back a sob of fear and relief. It looked as if Troy was going to let her stay, at least for now. With trembling fingers, she unbuttoned her shirt and wrenched away the sopping wet fabric. It dropped to the floor with a loud *splat*. Shivering, she drew on a flannel shirt two sizes too big. Next, she pulled off her drenched riding skirt and boots, and drew on the pair of britches Troy had provided. She rolled the cuffs clumsily above her ankles and straightened up.

Still shaking with cold, she clutched the waistband of the huge pair of pants and looked around. Spying a short length of rope lying in the corner, she snatched it up and threaded it through the belt loops on the pants. Gathering up her boots and wet clothes, she stuffed them under her arm and made her way back to the main room of the small cabin.

Betsy ran over to greet her. "Why is your face that funny color?"

"B-because I'm c-cold," Andi replied through chattering teeth. She dropped her wet clothes to the floor and fumbled with the rope, tightening it securely around her waist. Levi handed her a coarse woolen blanket, which she drew around her shoulders before huddling on the floor next to the fire.

"Look!" Betsy announced a few minutes later. "There's steam coming from your head." She giggled at the sight. "Are you cooking?"

"Leave her be," Troy snapped. He plopped down on the bed and glared at her from across the room. "Where's your horse?"

Andi clutched the blanket tighter around her shoulders. "She got scared in the storm and threw me. Then she ran off."

Troy slammed his fist against the wall. "That horse will head straight for home. Before morning, every cowhand on the ranch will be scouring the hills, looking for you." He rose from the bed and began pacing and muttering to himself.

"They probably already are," Andi said reasonably.

Troy crossed the room and grasped Andi by the shoulders. "Why couldn't you do what you're told?" He gave her a shake.

Hannah began to cry. She ran to Andi and threw her arms around her.

Andi looked over Hannah's golden head into Troy's eyes. "Justin said the children were my responsibility. I can't go home without them."

"That's what *you* think, my stubborn little sister-in-law. Just because I let you dry off in my cabin doesn't mean I'm going to change my mind. At first light, the kids and I are heading out. Without a horse, you'll be forced to either walk home or stay here. Either way, you won't be following us."

"You're going to Madera," Andi said, "to catch the train."

"How—?" Troy's face showed his astonishment. Then he nodded. "Think you're pretty smart, don't you? Well, so what? By the time anyone finds you, we'll be clean out of the state. Don't forget to give Katie my message."

"But the river! It's got to be high, especially after this storm. Hannah's so little. You—"

"Shut up!" Troy threw himself on the bed. He pulled a bottle of whiskey from under the mattress and uncorked it. "Another word, and I'll toss you out of here, storm or no storm. Understand?" He took a swig, corked the bottle, and stashed it under the mattress. "Now, I've had quite a day, so I'm hitting the sack." He pulled a hat from a nail overhead and covered his face. "Keep everybody quiet, m'girl, or I'll take a strap to you." He clasped his hands behind his head, let out a long sigh, and relaxed.

Before long, he was snoring loudly.

"Do you want something to eat?" Levi asked softly a few hours later.

Andi woke with a start. She lifted her head from the table without speaking. Although she was as warm as she could expect with bare feet and wet hair, she was weary beyond belief. Struggling through the storm had worn her out more than she had realized. After warming up at the fire and talking to Levi, she'd sat down at the crude table and laid her head across her arms, exhausted.

"Are you hungry?" Levi asked again. He placed a plate of cold beans and hardtack in front of her.

Andi nodded and picked up the fork. She forced the scanty meal down and turned to look at Betsy and Hannah. The girls lay curled in front of the fire on an old blanket. Another blanket covered them. They looked warm and cozy. Andi envied them. She wished she could close her eyes and sleep until she awakened and found this to be just a bad dream.

But she couldn't. Not tonight. She had a job to do, and she was going to do it. While Troy slept, half-drunk, she was going to gather the children and leave. She would take them back to Katherine if it was the last thing she ever did. Earlier, she had whispered her plan to Levi, and he had agreed to go along with it. "Justin said I was supposed to mind you, remember?" He grinned, and Andi knew that behind his cocky words, he wanted his mother as much as Betsy and Hannah did.

They had put the little girls to bed and stayed awake to make plans—until Andi fell asleep over the table. There really was no hurry. They couldn't do anything until they were certain Troy was sleeping soundly.

"When are we leaving?" Levi wanted to know. He glanced nervously at the figure lying on the bed. "It's way past midnight."

"When we're sure the storm's passed," Andi replied. Without a sound, she rose from the bench and approached the one tiny window. She cupped her hands to either side of her face and strained to see through the blackness. "The clouds seem to be breaking up. Perhaps there's a moon hidden somewhere behind them."

Levi came and stood beside her. "We're taking the horses, aren't we?"

Andi nodded. She didn't want to take them. They had a better chance of sneaking away and staying hidden without the added bother of getting the horses ready. But it was either take the horses or carry Hannah. She wasn't up to packing around a sleeping child. And besides, she didn't want Troy to be able to follow them when he awoke and found them gone.

She turned to Levi. "I'll get the horses ready. You stay here."

Levi nodded and handed Andi her jacket. She drew it on over the flannel shirt and crossed the room to retrieve her boots. They were still damp inside and uncomfortably cold. She shivered and made a face when she pulled them on. In spite of her fear of staying, she really, *really* hated to leave this cozy little cabin. With a sigh, she cracked the door. It slid open with only the whisper of a creak. Taking a deep breath, she slipped through the narrow opening and into the chilly night air.

Once outside, all the terror of her earlier experience that evening rushed over her like a flood. She pushed it aside and looked up. The clouds raced across the sky, revealing a few bright stars and a pale half-moon. It wasn't much light, but it served to show her the crude shed where the horses were stabled. She scurried around the three-sided building and peeked inside.

The horses were tied securely to a feed box. They looked desperately unhappy. Troy's large gelding danced and pulled at his rope until Andi could see the whites of his eyes in the pale light. She knew she'd have a difficult time keeping this huge animal under control in his present state. It would be madness to take him along.

She called softly to Patches and Coco. The two smaller animals nickered frightened greetings. She rubbed their noses and spoke gently while she untied them and led them around to the front of the cabin. No sooner had she taken them from the lean-to than a loud, insistent whinny pierced the air. She caught her breath and hurried back to the remaining horse. He appeared frantic to be let loose.

Why not? We can't ride him, and we can't leave him to alert Troy with his screams. Why not cut him loose and let him run? Putting thoughts into action, Andi approached the horse cautiously and freed him from his halter. With a snort and a whinny, he whirled around and sped off into the night. "Good riddance, and don't you dare come back," she whispered.

After tying Patches and Coco to a tree a safe distance away, she returned to the cabin. Slipping inside, she found a white-faced Levi staring at her.

"What's going on? Pa jerked in his sleep when he heard the horse scream."

Andi shot a panicked look in Troy's direction. He lay sprawled across the bed on his stomach, one arm dangling over the edge. He appeared to be in a deep sleep. "Your pa's horse didn't like being alone. I let him go."

"Let him go? Why?"

"He's in no state to be ridden. He's too spooked."

Levi sighed and followed Andi to where Hannah and Betsy lay sleeping. They had dressed the girls in their jackets and shoes before settling them in for the night. Now all they had to do was pick them up and carry them to the horses.

"You get Hannah," Andi said. "I'll try to wake Betsy."

Levi reached down. Blanket and all, he scooped his little sister and her doll up in his arms. She was heavy, and he staggered backward a few steps before catching his balance. Hannah didn't stir. Neither did Troy.

Andi opened the cabin door for the pair and turned back to Betsy. The little girl was too heavy to carry, so she bent down, covered the child's mouth gently with her hand, and whispered in her ear. "Come on, Betsy. Time to go home."

Betsy's usual response to the unexpected was a high-pitched shriek. Andi had heard it more than once during the past month, and she dreaded it now. Sure enough, Betsy sat up with a start and filled her lungs with air.

Andi held her hand tightly over Betsy's open mouth. "Be quiet."

Betsy's eyes were wide with fear and glassy from sleep, but for once, she obeyed Andi and closed her mouth. Andi snatched up the blankets, took Betsy's hand, and led her out into the night.

Levi wordlessly handed little Hannah to Andi and mounted Coco. Andi passed the sleeping child back to Levi, and he wrapped his arms tightly around her. He looked scared but determined. Hannah moaned softly, but then found her thumb and let out a contented sigh.

"How am I supposed to hold onto Hannah and stay on this pony at the same time?" Levi whispered in a shaky voice.

"Use your legs," Andi replied. "Grab onto his mane when you feel yourself slipping. I'll take his lead rope in a minute." She grasped Patches's mane and pulled herself effortlessly onto the horse's back. Then she reached down and dragged Betsy up in front of her. Gathering up the reins, she nudged the pinto. "Come on, Patches, let's go home." He responded instantly, to Andi's great relief. She took the lead rope from Levi's outstretched hand and turned Patches toward the old stage road.

They were on their way.

Chapter Seventeen

INTO THE NIGHT

I'm tired." Levi groaned and shifted the sleeping Hannah to a more comfortable position. "Hannah's slipping all over the place and I—" He yelped when Coco stumbled and sent him sliding off the pony's back and onto the ground.

Hannah landed on top of him and woke up with a shriek. "Mama!"

"This was a stupid, stupid idea!" Levi shouted up at Andi. He tossed Hannah aside and jumped to his feet. Hannah bawled. "We're lost," Levi continued. "I know we're lost. We've been riding around in circles for hours. I haven't seen or heard that creek you were talking about. It's starting to rain again, and I'm cold. I want to go back to the cabin."

Andi could barely see her nephew, even though he stood no more than a few feet away. The night had closed in around them when the clouds rolled in and covered the moon. With the pale light now hidden, the four children were plunged into darkness.

They had followed the old stage road for as long as Andi dared. Sooner or later she knew they had to leave it and set out over uneven, rolling rangeland, in order to get back to the ranch. The surrounding terrain was littered with brush, trees, rocks, and gullies—a dangerous route to travel in the dark—but it was the only way to go. She hoped they could find their way down to the creek soon after they left the road. Although it would take longer, they could follow the creek out of the hills and into the valley. Once on level ground, Andi was sure she could find the way home.

That was her plan, anyway. It was so simple. So direct. So sensible.

"So why isn't it working?" she grumbled as she listened to Hannah's sobbing and Levi's complaining. When they'd left the road, she'd led them slowly over the rough country, stopping every few minutes to listen for the sound of running water. After an hour, she still hadn't heard the familiar rushing of her favorite creek. She'd even given Patches his head, hoping he'd lead them home. If he was, she decided wearily, he was certainly taking the long way around.

Hannah continued to sob. Andi shook Betsy gently awake. "Betsy, wake up. I have to dismount and see to Hannah."

Betsy woke up enough to keep from falling off the horse. She yawned and clutched Patches's mane. "Are we home yet?"

Andi slid wearily from the horse and followed the sound of Hannah's wailing. Collapsing to the ground, she gathered the little girl into her arms and leaned back against a large boulder. She shivered and pulled the blanket around Hannah, drawing her close.

Levi shuffled over and sat down beside Andi, rubbing his eyes and yawning. "We're never going to find our way back. The rain will wash us away and nobody'll ever find us. Nobody."

At Levi's dire prediction, Betsy set up a wail. She threw herself from Patches and stumbled over to Andi. With a sob of terror, she shoved her way onto Andi's lap and wrapped her arms around her neck. "Don't let the rain wash me away, Andi," she pleaded.

Andi winced when Betsy's full weight came down on her legs. *What am I going to do? In a few minutes, I'll be crying, too. Are we really lost?*

In her heart, she knew Levi was right. She *was* lost. Perhaps in the daylight—if the sun came out—she could find her way home, but it was useless to tramp around in total darkness. She was so tired she'd soon be falling asleep on horseback.

"The rain won't wash us away, Betsy," Andi finally mumbled. "It's hardly coming down." She leaned her head against the rock and let the few raindrops hit her in the face. Closing her eyes, she sent up a quick, desperate prayer. *Lord, I know I'm in charge, but I don't know what to do. Please show me how to get out of this fix, so nobody gets hurt. Show me the way home!* Before she could finish her prayer, Andi found herself drifting off to sleep.

Levi's shaking roused her. "Don't go to sleep, Andi."

Is that the answer? she wondered. Aloud she said, "I don't think we can go any farther tonight. Even if we get soaked, we have to find someplace to rest."

"I'm for that," Levi said. He pointed into the darkness. "Is that a tree? Maybe we can crawl under it and get out of the rain."

Andi nodded. Together, she and Levi gathered up the two little girls and their blankets, and staggered to the dark outline of an old, crooked digger pine. It wasn't much shelter, but they crawled gratefully beneath the branches and curled up together for warmth. Within minutes, they were fast asleep.

Morning came, damp and dreary. Although the rain had stopped, water continued to drip steadily from the branches overhead. Andi opened her eyes and groaned. She felt terrible. Every muscle of her body ached, and she was cold and hungry. Worse, her throat hurt and her nose felt stuffy.

What do you expect from spending a night under a tree in the rain? She glanced down. Only the top of Hannah's head was visible. She lifted the blanket slightly and found Hannah curled up in a ball like a round, silky kitten. Next to her, curled up just as tightly, Betsy lay breathing softly. Both girls appeared none the worse for their all-night adventure. They looked warm and dry. Andi envied them. Her feet, especially, felt like chunks of ice in her cold and clammy boots.

She looked over at Levi. He was still asleep, his arm flung

protectively across his sisters' blanket. He shivered in his sleep, then rolled over and coughed. With a start, he sat up.

"Where are we?" he croaked, wiping the sleep from his eyes.

Andi shrugged. "Under that tree you found last night. I think it kept most of the rain off." Without warning, she sneezed. "I feel terrible. Let's get the horses and go home. I'm sure I can find my way in the daylight."

"Good." Levi nodded his head. "I don't feel so good myself." He coughed again. "And I'm hungry."

Andi pulled herself to her feet and looked around. A sinking feeling entered her hollow stomach. "I don't see the horses." She turned to Levi and swallowed. Her throat stung. "I don't remember tying them up. Did you?"

"Me?" Levi's eyes grew huge. "No. I didn't think about it. I was too tired. Didn't you?"

Andi shook her head. "I don't remember much about last night, except leaving the cabin." She let out a discouraged sigh. "Well, there's no help for it. I guess we walk."

"Walk?" Levi threw a glance at his sisters. "Them too?"

"Unless you're going to carry them." Andi stepped out from under the tree and turned slowly around. "If we're lucky, we might come across the horses later." She pointed toward a low rise in the distance. "I think the creek's that way."

Levi followed her gaze, turning a full circle. "Except for those tall mountains over there, everything looks alike. How can you tell one hill from another?"

She couldn't. The only landmark she recognized was the distant Sierra Nevada range, whose peaks were hidden under a veil of low, gray clouds. She knew, however, that the creek had to be somewhere in the direction she was pointing.

"Come on. The sooner we get started, the sooner we'll get home."

They roused the girls, to much whining and protest. When Betsy learned the horses were gone, she refused to move. Nothing Andi said could convince her to get up and walk. Finally, Levi reached down and jerked his sister to her feet. "Uncle Justin said you're supposed to mind Andi. Now start walking."

Betsy howled, but she did as she was told. Hannah picked up Tessie, stuck her thumb in her mouth, and reached out to take Andi's hand.

"We'll walk awhile, then rest. Then maybe I'll give you a piggyback ride." Andi smiled and shoved her still-damp braids aside. She picked up a blanket, wrapped it around her shoulders, and clasped Hannah's hand.

Levi took the other blanket and threw it around his shoulders. He grabbed Betsy's hand roughly and hurried to Andi's side. "How long do you think it'll take to get home?" A cough racked his body.

Andi sighed. "A long time. Maybe all day, unless we find the horses."

Levi groaned.

"Taffy's home by now," she added quickly when she saw Levi's hopeless expression. "I'm sure everyone's looking for us. They'll find us in no time."

Levi smiled weakly. "You think so?"

"Sure!" She didn't add how big the ranch really was and how it might take hours or even days to find four children wandering around the vast rangeland. She knew their only hope of discovery lay in following the creek.

The little group trudged on. They slipped and slid down brushy slopes into gullies, where water still ran from the storm the night before. Sloshing through the water, they made their way up the other side. Andi quickly decided that the ranch didn't look nearly as pretty on foot as it did from the back of a fast horse.

Walking became easier when the ground leveled off. Andi hoisted Hannah to her back. "Hang on."

"Giddy up!" Hannah squealed with joy. She clutched Andi around the neck and jostled up and down on her back. "Faster, horsey!"

Andi winced. She didn't feel very well, and Hannah was heavy. "I can't go any faster, Hannah. I'm a sick, tired old mare. I want to find my clean, dry stable and take a nap."

Hannah giggled. "Funny Nandi." She balanced her doll on the top of Andi's head. "Look, Levi. Tessie's riding too."

Andi gave Hannah a ride for a few minutes. When she could carry her no longer, she sank to her knees and set her down. "That's enough, Hannah. This horse has got to rest." She swallowed painfully and rubbed her itchy nose. Then she sneezed.

The children sat and rested. Levi was coughing longer and more often. He looked exhausted. Hannah laid her head in Andi's lap, and Betsy leaned against her shoulder.

"I wish I had a cup of hot chocolate," Betsy said wistfully.

"Hush!" Levi commanded.

Andi rushed to Betsy's defense. "You don't have to talk so mean to her."

"Shh!" Levi said, louder. He stood up. "I think I hear the creek."

Andi pushed the girls aside and leaped to her feet. She listened. "You're right. I hear it too. Come on." She grabbed Hannah and hurried toward the sound of running water.

A few minutes later, they stood on the banks of the swollen creek. Andi grinned. "I know exactly where we are now. We're upstream, about a mile from my favorite spot. All we have to do is follow the creek to my spot, then head for home. I know the way from there." She turned to Levi. "It's still a long walk, but at least it's easy going. And it's downhill."

Betsy's excited voice interrupted them. "Look!" She pointed. "A horse. Maybe we can ride."

Andi whirled in joy. Perhaps someone from the ranch had spotted them. Then her smile faded. She clenched her fists in alarm. "Oh no," she whispered, recognizing the horse at once. "It's Troy. His horse must have gone back. He's following us!"

Chapter Eighteen

No Place to Run

Andi dived behind a clump of scraggly willows and pulled the
girls down with her.

Levi fell to her side, breathing hard. "What're we going to do?"
He shook in fear.

"We're going to hide," Andi shot back. "I'm not letting Troy have
you—not after all we've been through."

"He's coming too quick," Levi said. "He'll find us and—and oh,
Andi! He's gonna be as mad as a peeled rattler for what you did."
Tears sprang to the boy's eyes and he threw his arms around her. "I
won't let Pa hurt you. I'll kick him if I have to."

Andi returned Levi's hug, then untangled his arms from around
her. "Don't worry about me. We'll hide real good." She lifted Hannah over a clump of scratchy bushes and motioned to Levi and Betsy.
"Get down here, as close to the creek as you can."

"These bushes don't make for much cover," Levi worried aloud.
He glanced briefly over his shoulder before hurrying to join Andi
and his sisters.

They huddled along the edge of the creek. Andi could feel it lap-
ping at her heels. She hoped they didn't fall in. As swollen as the
creek was, it could pull them away in a moment's time. She wrapped
her arms tightly around Hannah and held her close. "Nobody make
a sound," she said.

Peeking through the winter-dead brush a few minutes later, Andi
could make out Troy's horse trotting alongside the creek. She was

glad for the brush, as it made it almost impossible for Troy to bring his horse close to the creek at this spot. The undergrowth covered both banks for nearly a hundred yards up and downstream.

He'll have to dismount if he wants to search here, Andi thought. *If he does that, I'll circle around and snatch the horse. Then I'll gallop right over the top of him. That ought to surprise him enough to allow us to escape.* The thought made her smile.

Troy's voice startled her. "I know you kids are here. I saw you from the top of the rise. Now why don't you make it easy on yourselves and come on out?"

Hannah started to whimper, but Levi clapped his hand over her mouth. "So help me, Hannah," he hissed in her ear, "if you so much as peep, I'll—I'll take Tessie and toss her in the creek."

Hannah's eyes grew round at the threat. She swallowed her sobs and clutched Tessie tightly to her chest. She scowled at her brother and shook her head, but she didn't make another sound.

The four children lay next to the creek, flat on their stomachs. Dead branches poked them in their sides. Brambles caught in their hair. Water splashed over their feet and legs. Andi couldn't think of a more wretched hiding place.

For an instant, she considered standing up and showing herself to Troy. He'd be angry, all right, but he'd take Levi and the girls to a dry place. He'd probably leave her here to fend for herself, but anything would be better than lying in the cold, squishy mud. Her throat was on fire. Her nose was stuffed up so much she couldn't take a decent breath. Her head ached.

But she couldn't do it. She couldn't give the kids to Troy. She couldn't let Justin down. She would never be able to face Kate. Even God might be disappointed in her for thinking only of herself and how rotten she felt. She shook her head. No, she would not let Troy—

Without warning, she sneezed. Levi stared at her in horror. Andi closed her eyes, rubbed her nose, and willed the next sneeze to go away. It didn't work. As soon as she took her hand from her nose, she sneezed again. She couldn't help it. *Maybe Troy didn't hear it above the sound of the creek.*

There was a noisy snapping of branches, a muttered oath, and suddenly Troy stood above them, glowering. "I've about had it with you." He reached down and yanked Hannah to him. "Get up out of this muck."

Hannah screamed.

"You let her go!" Andi yelled. She threw herself at Troy's legs, which sent him crashing into the bushes. Hannah flew from his arms. "Run, get the horse!" she shouted to Levi. She held fast to Troy and watched the children scramble from the underbrush like frightened rabbits.

Troy shook Andi from him as if she weighed no more than a pebble. He lurched clumsily to his feet, entangling himself in the deadwood. Andi scrambled to her feet, grabbed Troy around the waist, and prayed for the strength to hold him long enough to give Levi and the girls time to mount up and ride away. *Hurry, hurry, hurry!* she pleaded silently. She didn't care what Troy did to her, so long as the children got away.

"You're nothing but a burr under my saddle," Troy muttered. He reached behind his back, grabbed Andi's arms, and jerked them free. Andi yelped. Then he gave her a shove that sent her stumbling backward again. She landed in the soft mud next to the creek.

Furious at herself for not being able to hang on longer, she clambered up the embankment and tried to knock Troy to the ground. "Don't you *ever* give up?" he bellowed. Turning to face her, he shoved her with both hands.

This time, Andi did not land in the mud. As she tried to regain her balance, she stumbled over a low-lying bush, hit the side of her foot on a rock, and tumbled into the creek. The shock of the icy, rushing water tore the scream from her throat. A second later, she was underwater, carried off by the swift current.

Unreasoning terror slammed into her mind as quickly as the swirling water closed in around her body. This creek was not the worn-out, muddy trickle from a month ago. This was a wild, raging flood. It slashed at her arms and legs when she tried to stand up. Her feet were swept out from under her before she could catch a breath of air. A large branch struck her in the face, but she was too frightened to feel the pain.

Flailing wildly, Andi managed to break the surface of the creek and gulp a breath of air. In that brief second, she realized she was traveling fast—faster than anyone could run. If she didn't reach the creek bank soon, she'd be well on her way out of the foothills and into the valley. But long before she reached the valley, she'd be dead. She was already so tired and cold; she couldn't fight the current much longer.

There would be no rescue this time. Troy wanted her out of the way, and he'd managed that pretty well. Besides, she was so far downstream he probably couldn't catch her even if he wanted to—and she was sure he didn't.

Andi managed to find the strength to pull in one more breath of chilly air. She tried to stand up, but just when she felt her feet touch bottom, the current snatched her away again. She was losing the battle. She knew it. She couldn't see anything but the foaming, muddy water. She couldn't hear anything but the roar of the creek devouring her. She didn't care. Not any longer.

Suddenly, a searing, ripping pain shot through her head. She gasped. To her surprise, her lungs didn't fill with water. The pain continued. Something was yanking on her hair, pulling her from the water. A moment later, strong arms caught her and dragged her from the freezing current. She winced as she felt herself dumped on the cold, soggy creek bank.

Andi immediately threw up. She moaned. Never had she felt so sick. She lay in the mud and gagged and choked, then threw up some more. Only when she had decided that she might live after all, did she open her eyes and look up at her mysterious rescuer.

"Fool kid."

It was Troy, breathing heavily and staring at her with dark, haunted eyes. He was soaked from head to toe. He planted his fists on his hips and growled, "You're nothing but trouble, Andrea Carter. If it wasn't for you, I'd be miles away by now. I should have left you in the creek."

Andi lay on her side, confused and freezing. She shook so much she could barely speak. "B-but you d-didn't leave me. You s-saved me," she said between chattering teeth. "Why?"

Troy reached down and lifted Andi into his arms. Then he settled her on his horse and climbed up behind her. "I don't rightly know," he admitted with a frown. "When I saw you tumble into the creek I just lit out after you." He grunted. "I'm sure I'll regret it." But he no longer sounded angry. Only tired, and maybe a bit frightened by what had happened. He nudged his horse into a trot. "Let's get back to the kids."

They rode in silence for a few minutes, with only the sound of the rushing water in their ears. Then Troy said, "You ruined all my plans, you know."

Andi said nothing. Even if she'd wanted to reply, she couldn't. She was too cold to do anything but clamp her jaw shut to keep her teeth from chattering.

Troy slowed his horse to a walk near a grove of trees upstream, where Levi and his sisters crouched under an oak. Levi had his arms around Betsy and Hannah, holding them close. All three were sobbing.

"Quit your blubbering," Troy said. He reined his horse to an abrupt stop. "Here she is, wet and cold, but alive." He dismounted and lifted Andi from the horse. Then he carried her over to the children and set her down.

Immediately, Levi wrapped a blanket around Andi's shoulders. He stood, rubbed away his tears, and faced his father. "Pa," he said in a trembling voice, "I'm not going with you. I'm staying with Andi 'til somebody comes for us. You can holler as loud as you like, or beat me, or try and drag me off, but it won't do no good. I'm not going. Neither are Betsy and Hannah. What you did to Andi ain't decent. She might've drowned. Kinfolk don't treat each other that way. If you want to be an outlaw, you go ahead. But leave us here." He reached around and snagged his father's hat from the ground and held it out. "Here's your hat."

Shaking with cold, and thoroughly miserable, Andi barely heard Levi's bold words. If Troy decided to take the children, there was nothing she could do about it any longer. She was too numb to care. All she wanted was a warm bed, a hot drink, and her mother.

Troy didn't say anything. He stood with his hands on his hips and stared at the bedraggled group huddled under the tree. He looked at Betsy. At Hannah. At Andi. Then he dropped his hands to his sides. His shoulders slumped, as if all the fight had gone out of him. He scowled at Levi. "You got yourself a mighty smart mouth, boy. But I reckon you're right."

Levi gaped. "Pa?"

"I got no choice but to leave you here." He didn't sound happy about it. "I saw for myself how fast the creek carried Andi away, so it's no good trying to cross the San Joaquin with you kids like I hoped. I'd be a fool to try. Chasing after you has cost me too much time, and I'm down to one horse." He shook his head. "Nope. I'll be lucky to save my own skin now. There's likely a poster or two with my picture on it hanging in some sheriff's office, so I'd best make myself scarce. I know when it's time to toss in my hand."

Troy snatched his hat from Levi, returned to his horse, and mounted. "So long, kids—for now. Tell your mother she ain't seen the last of me." He plopped his hat on his head and looked at Andi. "When I told you I didn't know how to repay you for pulling me out of the mud last month, you said I'd have done the same for you." He gave her a sudden, cocky grin. "Well, I reckon I did. We're square now. Paid in full."

Andi nodded her understanding. She tried to speak, but her thoughts were whirling. *He's leaving. He's leaving. Thank you, God! He's leaving the kids here.* Tears of relief and gratitude welled up in her eyes.

Troy turned his horse and headed back the way he'd come, toward old Millerton.

"Good-bye, Troy," Andi whispered. She watched until he and his horse were only a single moving speck in the distance.

Chapter Nineteen

FAREWELL

A ndi knew she was sick. It hurt to cough. And she was so cold. Although she lay under mountains of quilts, she shivered uncontrollably. *I feel terrible,* she thought. *Where's Mother?*

She didn't remember how she'd come to be lying in her own bed, but she knew somebody must have found her and the others shortly after Troy rode off. She vaguely recalled falling gratefully into somebody's arms. Chad's? Justin's? A ranch hand's? Her memory was a jumble of mixed-up images. It didn't matter. It was enough to wake up and find herself home at last, home where she could get warm and dry. She remembered taking a hot bath and going to bed. How long ago had that been? And why did she still feel so lousy?

"Andi . . ." Katherine's voice called her gently from her fevered thoughts.

She opened her eyes. Her sister stood above her, smiling. She held a covered tray in her hands. "Do you feel like eating?"

Andi shook her head and coughed. It was harsh and deep.

Katherine's expression turned worried. "I want you to try a little of this soup. Nila made a huge pot of chicken broth for you and Levi."

"How's Levi?" she croaked.

"He's sick too, although he's recovering faster. You both came down with bad chest colds. Dr. Weaver hopes yours doesn't turn into pneumonia."

"Where's Mother?"

"She'll be up directly. Right now she's resting."

Andi coughed again. "How long have I been sick?"

"Four days," Katherine replied. "But this is the first day you've been awake long enough to give me trouble. The rest of the week you drank your broth and took your medicine like a good girl."

"Four days!" She tried to sit up. "Are Betsy and Hannah all right?" Coughing again, she fell back against her pillow.

"They're fine," Katherine assured her. "Runny noses and all."

"Justin's going to have a fit. He told me to take care of the kids." Hot tears began to trickle down her cheeks. "I didn't do a very good job. I tried. I followed Troy and we escaped, but when I fell in the creek I knew it was the end. I couldn't do anything more. I was too cold. I sat under a tree and didn't care what happened anymore."

Katherine set the tray aside and sat down on the bed. "You're wrong, Andi. Justin's proud of you. And I'm so grateful. We heard the whole story from Levi. Every last detail. You didn't give up. I've sat by your bedside these four days and just thanked God for you and prayed for you to get well."

"What about Troy? Has anyone tracked him down?"

"I heard that the sheriff was interested in asking him some questions, so a posse went after him. They tracked him north of the river, but then the trail gave out. Nobody knows where he is."

"Are you—are you glad he got away?" When Katherine didn't answer, Andi blurted, "*I'm* glad. That sounds awful, doesn't it? But after he rescued me from the creek, he seemed different somehow, at least a little bit. He acted more like 'T. J. Silver' and less like 'Troy.' Maybe he'll straighten up and turn himself in. God sure straightened *me* up in a hurry last spring. I bet He could do the same with Troy, if only Troy would give Him a chance. Don't you think?"

Katherine picked up one of Andi's hands and gave it a squeeze. "Oh, I hope so, little sister. I really do."

"Good-bye, Levi," Andi said two weeks later, standing with him at the Fresno train depot. She had already hugged and said good-bye to Betsy, Hannah, and even Tessie, who still wore the "lecklace" Andi had given to Hannah. "I wish you'd stay for Christmas. It's only a week away."

"Aw, Andi. Don't start that again," Levi pleaded. "You know Mama promised Aunt Rebecca we'd spend our first Christmas with her in her fancy house in San Francisco." He shrugged. "I hear she's a lonely old lady, just waiting to spoil three little kids."

"Aunt Rebecca will spoil you, all right." *And hopefully she'll stop nagging Mother about me.* She reached out and threw her arms around her nephew. "I'll miss you. Come back next summer and you can be a ranch boy. Chad says I'm too old to hang around the hands all day." She grinned. "I bet Chad'd pay you, too."

Levi backed away and smoothed his new suit. "Don't start acting like a sissy girl. No mushy stuff." He crossed the platform. "When's the train coming, Mama? If it doesn't come soon, Andi's gonna talk me into staying and becoming a cowpoke."

Katherine laughed. "You'd make a good one, son. Your uncles have taught you a lot in the short time we've been here."

"You'll come back for a visit real soon, won't you, Kate?" Andi asked. "I'm going to miss you." She shook her head and grinned. "I never thought I'd hear myself say *that*. I can't believe I used to wish you hadn't come back."

Katherine drew Andi into a warm embrace. "It's all right. We all do things we regret and have to ask forgiveness for. You only have to look at my life to see that. My biggest regret is that I didn't come home sooner and make things right."

The distant sound of a train whistle cut through the air.

"I guess this is good-bye," Katherine whispered to Andi.

Andi nodded and backed away from her sister. "I love you, Kate."

When the train pulled out of the station twenty minutes later, Andi stood with the rest of her family and waved good-bye to Katherine and the children. *It's not really good-bye*, Andi decided. *They're not that far away.* She watched the train gather speed. The cars looked dark against the glowing winter sunset. *With Kate and the kids in San Francisco, maybe it wouldn't be so bad to visit Aunt Rebecca, after all.*

Then she grimaced. *What am I thinking?* But as she climbed into the carriage for the ride home, the words, *Well, maybe someday,* kept time with the steady beat of the horses' hooves.

To read more about Susan K. Marlow's adventures or to contact her, e-mail susankmarlow@kregel.com.

Circle C Adventures Book 1

ANDREA CARTER AND THE LONG RIDE HOME

ANDREA CARTER AND THE

Long Ride Home

Susan K. Marlow

HORSES, ADVENTURE, AND THE OLD WEST!

Twelve-year-old Andi Carter can't seem to stay out of trouble. Now her beloved horse, Taffy, is missing and it's Andi's fault. The daring young girl will do anything to find the thief and recover Taffy. But her choices plunge her into danger, and Andi discovers that life on her own in the Old West can be downright terrifying!